Gravity

(Wide Open Series - Book II)

SUNDAE LEIGHTON

Gravity (Wide Open Series: Book II)

Available in these formats:
- 978-1-7350077-3-1 (Paperback)
- 978-1-7350077-4-8 (eBook AZW)
- 978-1-7350077-5-5 (eBook EPUB)

Editing: My Brother's Editor
Cover: E. Leighton
Beta Reader: Stephanie Cooper

Chapter One

London

I pushed the fabric down on my bridesmaid's dress before I grabbed a glass of champagne from one of the waiters that happened to walk past me. No one was watching me at this moment, so I figured it was fine to have one glass. Sure, legally I was old enough to drink, but it didn't mix well with the medication I was on, but I really needed it to calm my nerves right now. I hated being out. I hated being social because when I was? I started to compare myself to all the other women in the room.

It didn't matter how many ED clinics, hospitals or specialists I saw. I was always going to think I was less than everyone else. It all started with one stupid kid in school telling me I was chubbier than the other girls, and I couldn't unhear it. For the past ten years, I have done nothing but worry about every single thing that I put into my mouth for fear that I would gain weight while I watched others eat without worry, and even though I desperately wanted to not be like that, it was harder than I wanted to admit. I wanted to be thin like the models I idolized but wanted to not care about that shit either.

My therapist said that I was getting better, but what the fuck did she know? Honestly, the woman went to school for this, but she had never danced with Ana or Mia like I had. Like my friends that I met at the last hospital I stayed at did. The last time I ended up in the hospital, which was three years ago, it had been the worst for me. I had starved and purged my way to noticed how thin you've gotten." Tears filled her eyes as she pressed her lips together.

"What happened?" I was suddenly mentally and physically exhausted as I tried to wrap my head around everything. This was not who I was, this was not who I wanted to be.

"You fainted." Brooklyn pulled the chair closer to the bed before she sat back down. "Lon, I love you, you're one of my best friends. You'd—" She stopped as she tried to get her thoughts together. "You would tell me if you had some sort of issue or problem, right?"

I nodded. "Of course, Sully. Absolutely." I lied right to my big sister's face.

That was just the beginning of my struggle with anorexia. I had just begun the long, deep fall down the rabbit hole. Things would only get much worse from this day forward.

Warning

This book deals with sensitive subject matter that may be difficult for some readers. Thoughts of suicide, eating disorder, self-harm, sexual assault and rape. Please do not proceed if this may offend or upset you.

If you or someone you know needs help with an eating disorder, please contact the National Eating Disorders Association at 1-800-931-2237 Monday through Thursday 9am-9pm and Friday 9am-5pm EST.

If you or someone you know is having thoughts of suicide, please contact the suicide prevention hotline available twenty-four hours a day at 1-800-273-8255.

If you or someone you know has been sexually assaulted please contact the sexual assault hotline at 1-800-656-4673.

If you or someone you know is in crisis, you can call the Hope Hotline at 1-800-442-4673.

Playlist

Paper Bag - Fiona Apple

A Thousand Years - Christina Perri

Sullen Girl - Fiona Apple

Gravity - Sara Bareilles

The Wave - Blake Shelton

Sangria - Blake Shelton

Fight Song - Rachel Platten

Stronger - Kelly Clarkson

Tied Together With A Smile - Taylor Swift

Try - Colbie Caillat

Warrior - Demi Lavato

I'm Still Standing - Elton John

Breathe (2am) - Anna Nalick

Hurt - Johnny Cash

Paint It, Black - Rolling Stones

Creep - Radiohead

Every Night - Paul McCartney

Mad World - Gary Jules

xanny - Billie Eilish

Pennyroyal Tee - Nirvana

Comfortably Numb - Pink Floyd

Still Learning - Halsey

Fix You - Coldplay

Die A Happy Man - Thomas Rhett

Perfect - Ed Sheeran

<u>Prologue</u>

London

Age 13

I reached up to pull my dark hair into a bun on top of my head as I felt the sweat trickle down my back. The ponytail from this morning was no longer cutting it in this hot, brutal July sun, and I suddenly wondered if I should have eaten more for breakfast before I pushed the thought away. Just the fact that my shorts were hanging off my hips while my shirt bagged around my stomach was enough to remind me that I was stronger than I ever thought possible.

The roar of the crowd brought my attention away from my body, and back to reality. I glanced over to where my older sister, Brooklyn, stood with her fiancé, Cooper Houston, as he waited for the NASCAR race to start. I wondered if Coop's brother, Finn, was around today. He and I were a few years apart, but I liked him enough. He was nice to me and he didn't try to touch me, unlike Cooper. My sister's fiancé was creepy with a capital C when it came to always trying to hug me or put his arms around me whenever she wasn't looking. Telling me how pretty I was, how big I was getting. I was thirteen. Not three.

"Be right back." Cooper pressed a kiss to Brooklyn's head before he rubbed my shoulder and disappeared into the garage. Gross.

Sully smiled at me. "Are you having fun so far?" Her eyes searched my face. "I know you didn't really want to come, but I thought it would be good for you to get out of the house this weekend since you've been spending a lot of time there lately."

We were close, Brooklyn, and I, despite the age difference. We had the same shitty mother who dumped me off with our grandparents when I was still in diapers, and Sully was ten years old. She always looked out for me, made sure to include me when she could, and was a great sister. She was the person I wanted to be when I got older, but I knew I would never be as good as Sully was.

"Sure," I told her even though I wanted more than anything to be home. Over the past few months, I had become a recluse of sorts, but that was because of my eating disorder. Because of the comments a few kids had made at school about my stomach and hips one day when they thought I wasn't listening. I never liked the way I looked before that moment, so I always tried to hide myself when we had to change in the lockers, making sure I wore baggier clothes. They apparently weren't baggy enough.

Brooklyn tilted her head as her hand came up to smooth a piece of hair from my face. "Really? Because you've been acting differently lately which I know happens with teenagers." A smile tugged at her lips. "Ask Grandma someday about how moody I was when I was your age." She giggled like we were sharing an inside joke.

"Really, Sully, you don't have to worry," I lied.

Brooklyn opened her mouth to say something else, but Cooper appeared again, so I was off the hook for now. I looked up to her and wanted to be like my sister. She was going to be this amazing photographer someday while she was married to this famous NASCAR driver.

She was flawless with her gorgeous chocolate brown eyes, and dark hair that matched mine, but never seemed to get frizzy or messy. We ran together in the morning when we could, but she always seemed to be able to eat whatever she wanted while I worried about every calorie that touched my lips. It was obvious we were sisters, but our bodies were completely different.

Brooklyn had curves that the guys loved while I had the kind they made fun of. Where my sister was easygoing and relaxed, I was shy and anxious. She had the most amazing eye for photos while I struggled to find my balance with school and life. Our grandparents never put pressure on either one of us, but for some reason, Sully always seemed to know what she wanted to do with her life while I felt confused and unsure of everything.

I sighed softly as I watched a few of the other drivers stop to talk to Cooper for a few seconds. I didn't follow racing even though my soon to be brother-in-law was a driver, and wondered as he introduced me to them, if maybe it was time. I had no idea about any of the logistics of the race or the sport itself, but never thought it was a big deal until today. Not until he showed up.

I blinked as black dots appeared before my eyes, but they quickly disappeared. Like I said, I never paid too much attention to NASCAR or the drivers, but he was different. He had dark hair and olive skin like a Greek god while his eyes were so dark *that they appeared almost black. My heart was beating so fast, and so loud, I was sure everyone could hear it.*

"Mason, this is London, Sully's little sister." Cooper jutted his chin in my direction. I was never more than Sully's sister to him when others were around, but he always made sure to introduce me.

Mason, even his name was perfect. I was already sweating, but I swear my pores broke open even more at the sight of the smile he flashed my way. "Hello." That was it, that was the one word he said to me, and I was head over heels for the guy.

Neither of them paid any more attention to me after that, but it didn't matter to me. I took in every single inch of Mason while he stood there, and I knew I needed to find out as much as possible about him. His car number, his sponsor, fuck I didn't care. Mason left a few minutes later to go to his car, while I stood there daydreaming about him. I wasn't fazed at all by the invocation of the race, the singing of the national anthem or when the drivers started their engines.

Brooklyn nudged me slightly to let me know we had to move away then, and I stumbled a bit. The heat was really starting to get to me. I felt like I was suddenly suffocating from everything. I reached for my sister, but at that point, it was too late.

I had already passed out.

When I woke up, I was in the medical center of the racetrack while Brooklyn sat next to me with a terrified look on her face. The moment she saw that I was alert, she sprang to her feet. "What the hell, London," she hissed at me. "Don't think I haven't needing a feeding tube inserted into my stomach. If it wasn't for my sister Brooklyn's ex-boyfriend, I wouldn't be here.

"Hey, London, how are you?"

Speak of the devil; did he know I was just thinking about him? I turned to find Rand Shepard, my sister's ex, standing behind me. His face was a mess of bruises and cuts, which made me gasp in surprise. "I'm good, but have you taken up boxing as a secondary job, Rand? You look like shit." I reached for another glass as another waiter walked by.

A smile tugged at his lips, but it didn't meet his eyes. "I've been busy." Rand took the glass from me. "You shouldn't be drinking." He tossed the alcohol back like it was nothing before he placed the empty flute down on the table.

I rolled my eyes. "It's a wedding, Rand; we should be dancing, having fun, and celebrating. Our friends just got married," I reminded him.

We were at the wedding of Brooklyn's best friend, Harper Rose, and Lake Mills, who was also a NASCAR driver like Rand. I happened to be a bridesmaid while Sully was the maid of honor. I had known Harper my entire life, so she was pretty much my other sister. For her to fall in love as fast as she did with Lake, and marry him? It was crazy, but I was happy for them. Harper had saved Lake's life, or so I heard from everyone, while he put her on a pedestal like the queen that she was. Alright, I'm kidding about the last part. The two of them fell madly in love which surprised us all.

"Right, but that still doesn't mean that you can get drunk," Rand said in his best grown-up voice. He was only two years older than I was, but he had clearly lived a harder life than most of us knew. His reputation for being a bad boy was well known. Everyone knew all about Rand, and his best friend Mason Pelletier.

I had had a thing for Mason ever since I had met him, but I hadn't spoken to him since that day. I was a bit of a closet NASCAR fan, but I followed all the races when I could, and tried to keep up with everything that was going on. I wondered if he was coming to the wedding, but hadn't actually asked anyone. Brooklyn would kill me if I went anywhere near him.

"You're kind of boring." I pouted just as I spotted my sister out of the corner of my eye. She'd probably kick my ass for talking to Rand but she was the one that had broken up with him. They had a lot of problems to work out, especially the one where she had his son without telling him. Not that I was going to get into that with him.

Rand's head spun around when he saw who I was watching. "Shit," he grumbled. "Has she ever talked to you about me?" His blue eyes were sad when he faced me again.

"What are we in high school now? Go talk to her yourself, Shepard." I watched as he reached for another glass of champagne. "Don't go getting drunk because that's not the way to win her heart," I reminded him.

"Point taken, little Sullivan."

I grimaced at the nickname Brooklyn's late fiancé had given me years ago. I hated it, but I was never able to seem to get away from it. "Could you not..." I let my voice trail off as I watched Mason walk into the room with a tall, leggy blonde on his arm.

Fuck, that had to be the infamous Apple with him. The man was a walking, talking Instagram model with that chiseled body and it was being wasted on *her?*

Rand chuckled. "You in there?" He waved a hand in my face before he moved his body to block my view. "Shit, London, you can't be serious." He shook his head as we both watched Mason brush the hair from the blonde's shoulder before he whispered something into her ear.

I hated her. I hated her for being with the man I had been dreaming about for years, and I hated her for breaking up Brooklyn and Rand. She had nearly ruined my sister, and if I could take away her pain, I would.

I squared my shoulders as I looked up at him. He had a big grin on his face. "What?" I asked.

"Nothing, but you should stay away from Mason," Rand told me. "He's not boyfriend material nor is he husband material." He touched my arm. "You're a sweet kid, and I would hate to see you get hurt because of him, even if he is my best friend."

"I'm not looking for a boyfriend."

"I can introduce you to some nicer drivers."

I didn't want nice, I wanted Mason. I had wanted Mason Pelletier since I had first laid eyes on him and had even thought about saving my virginity for the man, too, but that didn't happen. I didn't tell Rand that part though. "That won't be necessary." I started to move away from him, but he caught me by the elbow. I looked down at where his hand was before I looked up to meet his eyes. "Please let go of me," I warned. I hated being touched, no matter who it was. Sex was one thing, but hugs, handshakes, or even fist-bumps were altogether different.

Rand's hand fell to his side as he shifted his weight from one foot to another. "Do you want me to talk to Mason?" He had a gleam in his eye that told me I shouldn't listen to him, that I should run as far away as possible. "Because I can get Apple away from him, but you have to do something for me."

I folded my arms across my chest. "If you think that I can get my sister to talk to you, you better think again, pal." Brooklyn had ended their relationship after she thought Rand was cheating on her, and even though he swore up and down he wasn't, Brooklyn cut off all ties with him. Everyone had already tried to get them to talk, but that was over three years ago, and it still hadn't happened.

"Please, little Sullivan, I don't know who else to ask. Harper and Finn both tried, but she won't budge. You're my last hope." He pressed his hands together in prayer.

I snorted with laughter. "Stop it, Shepard, you and I both know that altar boy shit isn't going to work with me." I chewed on my bottom lip as I tried to figure out a way to get the two of them to talk. If Harper wasn't able to convince Brooklyn there was no way I could. I watched out of the corner of my eye as Mason moved to sit down with his date just as a thought occurred to me. "Can you get rid of her? Like, get her away from Mason? I can make my move once she's gone." I refused to even say her damn name.

"Duh."

"You have a son, Rand," I blurted out. Brooklyn would either hate me for the rest of my life for what I was about to tell Rand or thank me when she found out. I watched as his face went from shocked to angry, and then a weird calmness slipped over his features.

"Come again?" His voice was so low I could hardly hear it.

"Brooklyn had a baby nine months after you and she broke up. His name is RJ." I said a silent prayer that this would be the one thing that would work. Rand looked downright scary right now. "Wait until we eat, and everyone is ready to dance. Don't say anything until then even though I know it's going to kill you to wait that long." I watched as he slammed back another drink.

"Not a problem, London. I've been waiting this long, what's a few more minutes?" He raised his eyebrows at me. "I'll take care of Apple for you." Without another word, he turned and disappeared into the crowd.

Shit, what did I just do? My sister was never going to forgive me.

By the time everyone had eaten dinner, I was completely and totally wrecked. I couldn't believe I actually told Rand about his son. I felt like an asshole for blurting out my sister's biggest secret, but as my half-eaten plate was removed from where I was sitting I watched as Apple suddenly got up from where she was sitting, and disappeared. I located Rand who was standing at the bar with a drink in his hand, and he raised his glass at me before he took a sip. Everyone had started to get up to mingle with one another, so I took that as my cue.

I sprang from my seat to make my way over to where Mason was now sitting by himself. I was nervous as hell, but I could do this. "Hi." I sat down in the chair his date had just vacated.

Mason's eyes were the brownest I had ever seen in my life. It was like looking into the purest form of chocolate. I felt myself break out into a nervous sweat as he let his gaze move over my face, down to my chest, and back up to my face again. Sorry dude, but my tits are not where it's at. "Hello." His head tilted slightly.

"I'm London."

"I know who you are, baby," he informed me. "Not interested." It felt like a slap in the face, but I prayed it didn't show.

"Why not?"

Mason chuckled. "You're hot, London, don't get me wrong, but your sister will fucking cut off my balls if I lay one finger on you." He looked over his shoulder like he was making sure Brooklyn wasn't watching us before he turned back to look at me. "How old are you, little Sullivan?" A sly smile slipped across his handsome face.

"Old enough to know a few things," I advised.

Mason's brows dipped. "Trust me when I tell you that sounds very tempting, but we're bad for one another." He downed the rest of his beer before he placed the bottle on the table to stare at me with eyes the color of Starbucks dark roast.

"Why don't you meet me outside so I can show you how good

we may not be for each other?" I dragged my teeth across my bottom lip. "If you're interested, great. If not? That's your loss." I stood up and didn't look back as I sashayed my way across the dance floor. I made sure to put an extra swing in my hips because I knew that Mason was at least watching me walk away.

It felt like I waited outside forever. I thought for sure Mason would have followed me right out the door because everyone knew he was known to love his pussy and beer.

"What can I do for you, little Sullivan?" Suddenly Mason appeared out of thin air as he leaned against the side of the house where I had been waiting. That same sexy smirk on his face was back as he let his eyes wander all over my body again.

I didn't say a word as I stood up onto the tips of my toes, grabbed onto the tie he had hanging loosely around his neck and pulled his face toward mine. I had been waiting a very long time for this *exact* moment. To kiss Mason's perfect mouth and the moment we made contact, the air crackled with electricity.

A low growl came from deep inside Mason's chest as his hands came up to angle my head for a deeper kiss while I pressed my body against his strong one to get closer. I felt his tongue flick against mine and my core clenched at the thought of what he could do to me. Of where this might go. God, please let this go where I wanted it to.

"We can't do this, London." His lips fluttered against mine, but he didn't try to pull away.

"We can," I assured him as the kiss continued. I pushed my frame against his. "Don't you dare stop," I warned.

As the kiss began to build in intensity, I lifted my leg and

Mason grabbed it only to wrap it around his waist. "You're a naughty one, aren't you, little Sullivan?" He grunted as he nipped at my bottom lip.

"Hey, asshole! Get away from my sister!"

I pulled back to find Rand and Brooklyn standing there watching us like a couple of perverts. Except my big sister was flipped over Rand's shoulder caveman-style which meant he probably had to do that to get her to talk to him, but at least they were finally talking, right? Well, it looked like my job was done.

"See," Mason hissed before he pushed my leg back down. "Your sister is not exactly my biggest fan."

I tugged on his tie. "My sister is not the boss of me, Pelletier. I am not a fucking child and I want to fuck you." The words were out of my mouth before I could stop them.

His eyes went round and I watched as his pupils darkened with desire. "You're messing with fire, baby." He tried to pry my fingers from his tie, but I held on tightly. "Let go of me right now before you make me do something you're going to regret."

"Is that a threat or a promise, Pelletier?" I reached down and grabbed his cock, which was one hundred percent rock *fucking* hard. Not to mention fucking huge. Okay, maybe not as big as the rumors claimed, but bigger than anything I had felt before. I felt myself grow embarrassingly damp and slick between my legs at the thought of what he could do to me.

"You like what you feel, little Sullivan?" Mason chuckled. "Yes, I'm hard for you. You're a beautiful girl and I would be crazy not to be." His hands slipped up and over my ribs before he ran them up over my chest. I bit back a moan when he brushed over my nipples. "Is this what you want? Is it? You want me to suck on these little nipples? Fuck you with my big cock? I can do that, but that's *all* I'm going to do." He landed a punishing kiss against my mouth and pushed his tongue between my lips. Our tongues slicked together as one of his hands found its way down the front of my dress.

Mason wasn't gentle or easy. He was downright aggressive as he tugged and fondled me and his mouth ravished mine. My brain turned to complete mush, and I loved every single second of it.

"I'm yours." I breathed into his mouth and dug my fingers into his dress shirt. I wasn't afraid to let Mason take complete and total control of my body or the situation. After all, I'd been waiting for this moment a long time.

"Not here." Mason groaned as I rubbed against his thickness. "Not inside the house either. Come with me." He grabbed my hand and we started toward the cars.

Was he taking me to his place? My skin felt like it was on fire as I thought about what it would be like to visit his home or what it would be like to see his bed.

Mason dug his keys out of his pocket and I heard the beep-beep of the fob as he unlocked his car. The fact that he didn't even open the door for me shouldn't have been a surprise, but I wasn't looking for a boyfriend, I was looking to get laid. I climbed inside and then Mason grabbed me to pull me up into his lap.

"I can fuck you here," he whispered as he slowly kissed down my neck. "I can push this dress up over your hips, London, and fuck that tight little cunt until you cream all over my cock." His teeth grazed my skin.

Holy shit. I whimpered at the contact. "Do it." I tangled my hands into his dark hair. "I don't care where, just fuck me." He licked across my chest and I trembled at the contact. I was going to come before he even got inside me.

"Is that what you want?"

I dropped my hands so that I could tug on his zipper. "What I want, Pelletier is you inside me," I whispered. "If it's here, in your car? Then yes that's what I fucking want."

Mason grunted at my words, and then he lifted his hips so that he could pull down his pants. I looked down to get a good look at his dick. Holy shit, it was fucking huge! There were rumors about Mason, about his porn star sized penis, and they were all fucking true. He had to be a solid nine inches from the looks of it. Not that I knew a lot about penises, but I'd seen my fair share over the years. A lusty feeling of warmth began to pulse throughout my body before animal hunger took over.

I shifted slightly so that I could yank my dress up over my waist. Then I pushed the fabric of my underwear to the side, and just as I pressed the wet entrance over the head of his dick, I met Mason's eyes.

"You sure this is what you want, London?" His eyes were wild. "There's no taking this back once it's over."

"Do you think I'm some sort of virgin?" Instead of letting him answer, I dropped down on top of Mason and threw my head back as pleasure pulsed throughout my entire body. I could feel him stretching me, filling me, and I needed more before I self-combusted. I cried out as I eased myself back up onto my knees only to lift back up and, fuck, he was *everywhere*. I could feel Mason all over my body as we fucked, because that was what this was. Straight up fucking.

"Shit." Mason gritted his teeth as he gripped my thighs to pull me closer. His hand suddenly wrapped around my hair and he pulled it into a knot as we moved together.

I met his eyes as we moved. I was afraid if I made a sound I would scream so loudly everyone inside would hear me. Every single thrust sent me reeling as pleasure racked my body and I was sure I was going to wake the dead when I finally came.

"Little Sullivan, you feel like fucking heaven." Mason's hips met mine. "I thought for sure you would be a virgin." He pressed his mouth against my neck.

I whimpered as he hit me in places I had never felt before. "Not a virgin," I told him, although I had planned on saving it for him until I couldn't. I was surprised at how my body just sucked him back in, held him so fucking tightly. "Just a girl that—*oh my god.*"

My orgasm hit me from out of nowhere the moment Mason wrapped one of his hands lightly around my neck. It wasn't tight enough that I couldn't breathe. Just enough pressure to make everything catch on fire. Heat streaked through me as his mouth found mine to capture my screams. I could feel him coming with me as he held me down against his hips, and then I came again when he did that as his shaft dragged over my clit. My eyes rolled back into my head as I rode out my second orgasm, and then I came a third time before I was done.

"Jesus Christ, London." Mason panted when I started to pull away from him. "What the fuck was that?"

My eyebrows dipped as I climbed back into the passenger's seat. "Sex?" I adjusted my underwear before I pulled my dress down. I felt like I had just run a fucking marathon, but I needed to play it cool, and not act like some young girl with a crush. Which is exactly what I was.

"Funny." Mason ran his hand through his hair and then down the back of his neck. "I've never had a girl come like that before." His lips turned up.

"You've never made a girl come before?" I teased as I watched his face.

Mason threw his head back and laughed. I felt something funny rip through my chest when he did that. The sound was amazing. "That's not what I meant, little Sullivan. I meant the way you came. It was the hottest thing I've ever seen." He tucked his junk back into his pants before he spoke again. "You want to go inside now that your sister is gone? We can dance or whatever." The look of something I couldn't put my finger on flashed in his eyes but disappeared before I could read it.

I shrugged. "What about your date?" I wasn't about to forget about Apple.

"Apple?" His eyebrows shot up. "What about her? She's not my date." Mason leaned closer so that his breath warmed my face. "You can say no, little Sullivan. I'm sure I can find someone else to occupy my time."

I opened my door. "Let's go back inside." I started to climb out of the car, but then Mason's hand gripped my arm as he tried to pull me back inside. It wasn't sex anymore, so I didn't want him to touch me now. Touching was for fucking only. I began to sweat as I resisted the urge to rip away from him.

Mason smiled. "Something tells me you're used to being bad, aren't you?" He must have seen something in my face or my body language because he suddenly released me.

I stepped out of the car, but leaned my head back inside. "How about we go inside, dance a little, get drunk, and see what happens?" I waited for Mason to climb out so that we could walk inside together, not caring who might see.

Yet, if I had known what was going to happen next, I wouldn't have suggested that. I would have stayed as far away from Mason Pelletier as possible.

Chapter Two

London

Here's the thing about having a one-night stand. You're not supposed to see them again. Which is what I thought was supposed to happen after I slept with Mason. After we spent an hour or two dancing, kissing, and rubbing up against one another at Harper and Lake's wedding, we went back to my hotel room. I woke up alone the next morning, which honestly didn't surprise me. The only thing that Lake left me was a fondness for having my hands tied together, and a few bruises that I knew would fade after a few days.

The only problem was that right now we were currently staring at one another across the reception of Brooklyn and Rand's wedding. That's right, my sister *just* married Rand Shepard, just a few weeks after he found out about their son. Turned out they both still loved one another, and since Rand almost fucking died in a car crash less than forty-eight hours ago, he decided he didn't want to wait another minute to marry her.

I honestly felt like this was one of the most awkward things I had ever had to deal with. Should I pretend that I don't know him or that nothing happened? Or did we *talk* about what happened? I had never actually *had* a one-night stand before. My hand automatically went up to the silver heart that dangled from the chain around my neck, and I played with it as I watched Mason start to walk toward me. I'd be a liar if I didn't think about bolting from the room right now.

As always, Mason looked like he fucking owned the fucking place. His dark hair was perfect while his thick, muscled body was nearly bursting from the tuxedo he was wearing after being the best man. His eyes didn't move from my face as he came to a stop directly in front of me and licked his cupid lips before he spoke. "How have you been, little Sullivan?" Mason smiled for a second before he dropped his eyes down my body.

"Fine." I started to move around him, but Mason blocked my path. "What, you want to make small talk now? Talk about the weather or maybe do one another's hair?" I tried to keep my voice strong, but it wobbled slightly.

Mason broke into a big smile that showed his teeth. White, straight, and perfect teeth which made me wonder if he had braces as a child or maybe they were veneers. "I like how you think, London." Mason's hand came up so that he could use his knuckles to tilt my head and forced me to make eye contact. He brushed his thumb across my bottom lip before he pulled it down lightly. "What I wanted to know was if you wanted to fuck." His voice was thick with need.

I tried to keep myself from showing any emotion, but by the way Mason raised one eyebrow at me that clearly wasn't the case. "I-I—" I needed to get away from him. This wasn't how I had planned things. I *always* planned everything out, and Mason fucking Pelletier was trying to ruin that.

"Cat got your tongue, little S?"

I narrowed my eyes. "You need to get your hand away from me, and let me by," I warned him. "We had our fun, but that was then." I tried to go around him again, but Mason once again stopped me.

"What's your deal?" He growled between clenched teeth. "You're fine with touching when it's sex, but otherwise, what? You got some germ thing going on, little Sullivan?"

"Back the fuck off and stop calling me that," I warned him again. I fucking hated that nickname. The only person I let get away with it was Harper, and that was only because I was kind of scared of her. "Let me pass or I'll—"

"Or what, London? Scream? Ruin your sister's wedding? You sure you want to do that?" Mason pushed. "She hates me enough, but I'm sure you freaking the fuck out right now would really put you on her favorites list." His eyes gleamed as he dared me.

Shit, the guy was right. I wouldn't, not after everything Brooklyn and Rand had done for me. Schooling, hospitals, and numerous other things both of them had taken care of for me since I got myself into this mess. "Leave me alone." I managed to get away this time, but I could hear his footsteps as I went out into the hallway. Should I run? Would he just follow me? I spun around. "Stop fucking stalking me!" I glared.

"You're making this too easy." Mason smirked. "I won't chase you if you don't want me to, London." He held up his hands. "Just tell me you don't want me again, and I'll leave." He took a step back and folded his arms over his chest. I half expected the buttons on his shirt to pop off as they strained against the fabric.

Of course if I said I didn't want him that would be a lie. I knew sleeping with Mason again would be a mistake because it looked like we would be seeing one another a lot more now that my sister and his best friend were married. "We shouldn't," I whispered as I felt my body tremble at the memory of what it had felt like with Mason inside of me, and how many orgasms he had given me.

"Why is that, little Sullivan?" Mason suddenly had me pinned against the wall, and despite the fact that we both knew someone could catch us at any moment, we didn't seem to care. He pressed his very hard body against me as he leaned down to whisper into my ear. "You didn't enjoy multiples? Did it not feel good when I was inside you because you felt fucking amazing wrapped around me, baby." He nipped on my lobe as he ground himself against me. "I'm not asking you to be my wife, just asking you to let me come inside you." He nibbled at the skin as he slowly worked his way down my neck.

I bit back a whimper as Mason cupped my sex with one hand and began to slide the skirt of my dress up with the other. What was it with us and weddings? I felt the air hit my skin just as Mason's fingers dipped under my underwear, and he groaned into my neck when he found just how much I *did* want this.

"Little Sullivan, you are a slippery fucking mess. Don't lie to me. Tell me you want me." Mason's thumb grazed my clit enough to make me want more. No, I needed more, and he knew it.

"I want you."

Mason pulled his head back to look at me. "Say it again." He ran his tongue around the seam of my lips. "Tell me you want me to fuck you, little S." He wiggled his finger, and I closed my eyes as pleasure flooded my body.

"I want you," I whispered. "I want you to fuck me, Mason."

Mason growled. "This way," he told me, and before I realized it, he had pulled me into the janitor's closet. "Tell me something." He reached behind me to slam the door shut before he turned on the light. "Is there anything you haven't done before?" His eyes were black as night when he turned back around to face me. "You avoided that question when I asked you before. So, tell me now." He started to unbuckle his pants.

"No." I swallowed hard. "There's nothing. I've been with a girl, I've been with two guys, and, yes, I've been with a guy, and a girl."

"Take off your dress."

I turned around. "You'll need to unzip me first," I instructed, and just when I thought he wasn't going to do what I asked, Mason's arms suddenly circled around my waist. He cupped my tits in both hands and licked around the back of my neck which caused me to shiver.

"There's nothing left, baby?" Mason whispered into my skin as his fingers found my nipples. "Nothing at all that I couldn't show you?" He started to lift my dress up as if he wasn't going to bother with removing it until the sound of knocking caused us both to freeze.

"You two had better get out here before Brooklyn sounds out the National Guard." Finn's voice boomed through the wood. "She's pissed off enough as it is, but if she finds the two of you together? All hell is going to break loose." He pounded on the door again. "I'm not leaving until you both come out."

"Shit." I hissed. "I told you—"

"Re-fucking-lax, London. We're both adults. Didn't you already tell me that before or something along those lines?" Mason was pulling his pants back up. "You go first, go with Finn, and then I'll just make my way in a few minutes later. Easy fucking peasy."

I rolled my eyes. "Sure." I put my hand on the door before I turned over my shoulder. "What were you getting at? Before, the whole never tried anything shit?" I tilted my head as he grinned at me in the dark as I flipped off the light.

"You'll have to wait to find out, won't you?" Mason winked.

"Asshole." I pulled the door open to find Finn standing there with his hands on his hips. When I was younger, before Mason, I had a small crush on Finn. He was only a couple years older than I was, but now that just seemed like eons ago. He was still good looking with his dark curls and green eyes, but now he was more of a brother to me than anything else.

"You two done?" Finn didn't try to touch me, but I could see the anger flash in his eyes. "Knock the shit off." He warned Mason before he looked at me. "You don't need to get involved with him, Lon, you have your entire life ahead of you."

"Thanks for having my back, man. Appreciate it." Mason barked from behind me. "It's not like I'm going to corrupt the girl or anything. Think that was already done before I got involved."

I shot a look at Mason. "Enough. Both of you. Let's just get back to the wedding reception." I started walking before either one of them answered and figured they would follow me.

Brooklyn's eyebrows shot up when I walked into the room, so I made sure to flash big sis a huge smile as I headed her way. "Where were you?" Her voice was hushed. "You need to stay away from Mason Pelletier, do you understand me? You're doing great right now, London, getting involved with someone like him is only going to mess that up," she warned.

"Have you been talking to my shrink again?"

"Stop it." Brooklyn shook her head. "That's not what I'm talking about, and you know it. You're in recovery, you're in school, and you don't need to get involved with anyone. If you need to date, find a nice guy at college. Not a NASCAR driver."

"But, it worked out so well for you, and for Harper." It had, but not at first. Not for either one of them, but I was just trying to piss her off. She was doing the same to me right now. I wish everyone could stop treating me like a child, like they were my damn parent, and maybe more like my sister or a friend.

Harper's gray eyes flashed, but before she could say anything, I stopped her. "Look, I appreciate everything you two are saying, but I'm fine. Honestly." I flashed a fake smile their way. "Mason and I are not an item or anything. We're just—"

"Just?" Brooklyn's eyebrows dipped, and the wrinkles in her forehead caused me to instantly regret saying his name. Why did she hate him so much?

"Nothing, we're nothing," I assured my sister. "Why don't you go be with your husband?" I suggested as Mason walked back into the room. I probably wasn't going to be able to talk to him for the rest of the reception, but that was probably for the best right now.

Sully pressed her lips together. "Lon, I love you, that's all this is. You know that right?" She reached up to touch my cheek lightly before she smiled at me. "You'll thank me someday when this is your wedding reception." She looked like she might lean in to hug or kiss me, but changed her mind. "Now, I'm going to spend time with my man." Brooklyn giggled before she hurried off to join him.

Harper slipped off at the same time which left me alone. I knew talking to Mason was out of the question, but that didn't stop me from scanning the room trying to find him. He was in the corner with Watson Brooks and Hudson Fox, a couple of other drivers. I watched as he casually pulled his cell phone from his pocket before he locked eyes with me, winked, and looked down at his phone.

I needed some damn fresh air.

I made sure to grab my clutch on the way out which had my cell, not to mention a couple other essential items, before I pushed open the side exit door. I leaned back against the building and took a few deep breaths. Fuck, why did everything always have to be so damn hard? Why couldn't I be normal like everyone else instead of this fuckup? I pulled the half-empty pack of cigarettes from my bag and the moment the nicotine hit my lungs, I felt my anxiety slip away. My cell buzzed slightly and I realized I had several missed texts from a few friends from school as well as my best friend, Rush Powell.

Rush: *Still in NC?*

Rush: *Hello?*

Rush: *Are you ignoring me?*

Rush: *Did you hook up with Mason again?*

Rush: *Fine, don't give me deets.*

I shook my head as I started to text him back that I would call him as soon as I could until I heard a soft cough behind me. I dropped the cancer stick on the ground like a kid caught by her parents and spun around, making sure to stomp it out at the same time.

"Busted, little Sullivan." Mason grinned at me while his eyes gleamed with mischief. "I didn't take you for a smoker, but then again, you seem to surprise me more and more." He took a step toward me.

"You shouldn't be out here. We can't see one another again. I told you that already," I warned.

"Who are you texting?" He pointed at the phone in my hand. "Boyfriend?"

"What? No." I shoved my hand behind my back. "None of your business, actually. Why don't you go back inside before Sully or Finn or someone realizes we're both missing?"

Mason lunged forward like he was going to grab me, and that caused me to jump back. I nearly lost my footing, but he managed to hook his arm around my waist to keep me from going over. "Why are you keeping secrets?"

"We're not a fucking couple, Pelletier." I narrowed my eyes at him. "Why do you care?"

Mason glided his hand up the left side of my body, around my neck, and then to the back of my head. "Because I'm curious about you, London. You intrigue me. You came after me at Lake's wedding, and when I said no, you didn't give up. You didn't seem to care that I left the next morning, and when I came to you today? You didn't want anything to do with me." Mason's lips were so close now that I could kiss him if I wanted, and truth be told, I wanted to. "Are you lying, little Sullivan? Do you want me again, or are we done? Was it just wham, bam, thank you ma'am, or do you want me to fuck you again?"

My body betrayed me when I shivered, and I watched the way his eyes flashed with heat when he realized I wanted him as much as he wanted me. "You already know the answer to that question," I reminded him.

Mason smirked before he slowly ran his tongue around my jawline. "You're staying at Shepard's, right?" He nibbled at my chin.

"Y-yes."

Mason's lips brushed mine. "I'll see you tonight," he promised before he let go of me. "Who is he?" he asked.

I shook my head. "What?"

"Rush? Who is he?" Mason held up my cell phone, which he now held in his right hand.

"Son of a bitch! Give that back!" I tried to grab it, but he just held it away from me. "Seriously, Mason? How old are you?"

Mason chuckled as I jumped in these stupid heels trying to get my phone. "Just tell me, little S, and you can have your phone."

"He's just a goddamn friend, Mason. Jesus." I was going to lock my phone when I got it back. I should have done that a long time ago.

"Was that so hard?" Mason held out his hand so that I could

snatch my cell away from him. "When we're fucking, you're only fucking me. Do you understand? Rush had better just be the friend you told me he was. Not an ex or a fuckboy or anything like that." His voice was full of venom.

I resisted the urge to roll my eyes. "Whatever." I shoved my phone back into my clutch and nearly screamed when Mason grabbed my arm, flipped me around, and caged me against the wall face-first.

"I'm not kidding," Mason hissed into my ear. "You don't fuck anyone else when it's my dick you're riding."

"What about you? Do you get to stick your cock inside every cunt you want?" I fought back. He was going to bruise me, but I didn't care. I liked it rougher than he realized.

Mason turned me back around so that we were facing one another. I watched as his eyebrows dipped. "Such a dirty mouth, baby." He slid his lips against mine and then slammed his mouth over mine so hard I stumbled, but he caught me by wrapping his arms around my waist. His tongue swirled around before he slicked it against mine, and I moaned into the kiss as it went on. Fuck, the man was everything I always wanted when it came to things like this. Mason tugged on my bottom lip with his teeth so hard I tasted blood when he started to pull back. "Fine, London. My dick is yours right now." He smacked my ass. "I'll see you tonight."

I watched as Mason walked back inside the building, and then I waited to follow him back inside. I knew I was getting in over my head. Bringing him to my sister's house was really pushing the limit, but I couldn't say no to Mason now. He wanted me as much as I wanted him, and if he was going to only fuck me, then so be it.

Chapter Three

MASON

Call me an asshole, because that's totally what I am, but I didn't go see London like I said I would tonight. I knew that was going to be a problem the next time we saw one another, but that would be something I would deal with when the time came. I was struggling big time with the need I had to be inside London Sullivan again or to at least be near her. Why I even cared who the *fuck* she was texting when I found her outside the wedding reception when normally I didn't give a rat's fucking ass was beyond me. I couldn't figure out what it was about this girl that was pulling me toward her, and I wanted it to stop. *Now*.

I don't think I had *ever* met a woman quite like her before. London was a shot of whiskey that burned going all the way down. When you wake up the next morning, you swear to yourself you'll never drink like that again until you see her, and you have to have another taste, another drink. Why? Because London Sullivan was *worth* the hangover. She reminded me of me only times a million. You couldn't expect to contain a tornado, and I had no doubt that London Sullivan could not be contained. You could give it your best damn shot, but something told me that girl would break you in every single way imaginable.

I wasn't sure what happened to her to make her that way, but I knew what made me like this. Growing up, it was just me and my mother. My asshole of a father split before I was even crawling so Mom had to work a couple of jobs just to support the both of us. When she realized I was actually good at racing, she picked up a third job until she couldn't do that anymore and that's when my dear old grandfather, Henry, stepped in. That would be my mom's father, although he wasn't exactly the grandfatherly type. Mom's parents kicked her out when she got pregnant with me at fourteen, so she bounced around from place to place until she finally found someone that let us stay on their couch for a bit. Henry showed up when I started winning some go-kart races and all he could see was fucking dollar signs when he looked at me.

After that, well, we never had to worry much about money. No more sleeping on couches or living in homeless shelters. Henry had money. A lot of money that was from his grandfather and it was nice to have a roof over our head, food on the table, and clean clothes that weren't a couple sizes too big or too small. It was just in time, too, because it was right around then that Mom got sick. Henry was there to swoop in like some kind of fucking hero to make sure she got the best hospital care, medication and I was able to keep racing. I was lucky to have that because without it I wasn't sure how I would have survived. Mom was all I had and when she died, it was like a part of me went with her.

After Mom passed away, Henry didn't really seem to care what I did as long as I kept racing, kept winning, kept bringing in money and stayed out of his way. He sponsored my cars, he took me to the races, and he let me sleep in his house. I had no rules, no parenting and absolutely no one to make sure I stayed out of trouble, which I got into a lot of once the racing didn't help with my anger.

Until I met Layla.

Layla Green was my first taste of pussy when I was fifteen years old, and to this day I can still remember the way her tits looked as she bounced on my dick. The way her blonde hair brushed my thighs as she arched her back and the way she sounded when she came. Layla was my first for a lot of things that night. The first time I got drunk, the first time a girl touched my dick, my first blow job, and the night I lost my virginity. Hey, it wasn't for a lack of trying, but I guess I just needed a girl that had done it all before.

Layla was the same age as I was, and she sought me out after the race. Said she had a couple of cans of beer in her car if I was interested. With those dark eyes, those tits, and that ass of course I was interested. I was supposed to get a ride home from a friend, but that changed real quick once Layla got involved. Once she found a place to park, we had a couple of sips of that beer and she put her hand on my dick and asked me if I had ever had a real blow job before. It wasn't too long after that Layla stripped off her clothes, straddled my waist and fucked me. She had to tell me what to do in the beginning because I was a little stunned that this was actually happening while I watched her magnificent tits, but I soon snapped out of it. Layla liked her hair pulled, her ass slapped, and I gave her everything she wanted while she taught me more than I could say I did for her. I think she knew what she was getting into with me because she never complained. I still see her now, and again, too. She's married now with a couple of kids, but still has those great fucking tits.

After Layla, I chased after every single girl I saw. Once I got my dick wet, I couldn't seem to get enough. I was obsessed with pussy, with tits, ass, and the more I had, the more I fucking wanted. I soon learned that I could have a girl at every single track waiting for me so I didn't have to worry about finding one when they would come to me. Everyone thought Apple was my side piece at home in North Carolina, but she wasn't my girlfriend and she never would be.

But, London? London was different than any single girl I had met before. Sure, *she* came to *me*. I was used to that. But she didn't get clingy after the fact like others did. She didn't freak out the next morning when I left her hotel and tried to get my number or track me down, which she easily could have done. I knew she was young, and clearly had her own issues, but I actually fucking liked London. We had fun together at Lake's wedding after we fooled around, and when we went back to her hotel, I realized she was one of the kinkiest fucking chicks I had ever met, too, which is saying a lot. It didn't matter that London was young because it was clear to me that she had lived a thousand lives in her twenty-something years on this earth. I could tell by the way she didn't like to be touched unless it was sex or the way she pushed the food around on her plate when we had a little midnight snack that there was something going on in that head of hers.

I might like my women with issues, but London Sullivan was a special fucking edition that should come with a warning.

You might be wondering what did I end up doing instead of going to see London? It just so happened that I received a text message or rather, a picture via said text message, of a nice rack. I had no idea who it was because I didn't recognize the number. It turned out to be Annie, the nurse from the hospital I had to sweet talk to get Brooklyn into Rand's room the day he had a terrible accident, and so I went to her place instead. Right now I was watching her lips as they swallowed my cock over and over again.

Annie was fucking good at it, too. She gripped the base of my cock with her slim fingers while she slipped my dick down her throat. The entire thing, too, not just the head while she flattened her tongue against the underside of the shaft while she bobbed up and down. I grunted as I twisted my fingers into Annie's dark hair which only seemed to make her look up at me under her lashes.

"Mmmmm." Annie purred as she dragged her pink tongue around the tip of my dick. "You're so fucking big, Mason." She ducked her head back down to start sucking me off again, but I had other ideas. Better ones like sinking my cock inside that wet pussy all fucking night. Annie whimpered softly when I tugged on her hair to pull her face up to mine.

I watched as hunger pulsed throughout my veins while she stood up, and reached behind her back to unclasp her dark, red lace bra that hardly contained her tits. She dropped it to the floor as she stepped out of the matching panties. "You want me, Mason?" Annie was stunning with her thick, dark hair, and creamy skin. She pushed me back against the couch so that she could climb up onto my lap.

"Why don't you sit down on my dick so that you can find out just how much?" I wrapped a hand around my shaft and began to slowly pump myself while we stared at one another. I reached over to grab the condom I had dropped on the table next to the couch and carefully ripped it open to slip it on over my cock.

Annie dragged her teeth across her bottom lip as she watched before I helped lift her up onto my cock. Slowly, so fucking painfully slow, Annie eased herself down onto me while she kept her hands on my shoulders. I noticed she still had on her black heels, and fuck, that was sexy as hell. I smashed my mouth against hers as she slipped all the way down to my balls and I swallowed the moan that escaped from her lips.

"Holy shit." Annie pulled back to look into my face. Her eyes were wide as she moved, and she cried out as my cock stretched her wide. "I need you to fuck me. Can you do that? Can you fuck me really good?" Her voice shook as she arched her hips to ride me with rough, strong strokes.

I broke into a smile as I rolled Annic onto her back before I eased hcr thighs open. Then I threw her legs over my shoulders and slammed myself so hard into her that I swear I might have seen stars. "That's what you want, sweetheart?" I growled as sweat began to break out on my forehead.

"Harder, Mason, make me come."

I gripped on to Annie's hips as I pulled my cock all the way out of her slick pussy before I pushed all the way back in. I watched as her eyes went wide as she clenched around me, but I wasn't anywhere close to blowing my load yet. I pinched my eyes shut and gritted my teeth as I pictured London's face along with her body and what she felt like when I was balls deep inside her. Sobs of pleasure and the slapping of skin filled the room as I finally began to feel that familiar tingle creep up my spine.

Annie moaned my name which caused my eyes to fly back open. She arched her hips to match my thrusts and I watched as she came undone underneath me. She whimpered and cooed as she rode out the orgasm, but I wasn't going to be able to come now. The feeling was long gone. I buried my face against Annie's neck as I faked it for the first time in my life. I moaned and licked Annie's neck as I shuddered before I shifted to roll off her quickly so that I could pull off the empty condom. I tied it up and tossed it in the garbage.

"Should I go?" I asked after I came back from the bathroom.

Annie shook her head. "You can stay the night," she whispered. "No strings," she added.

I woke up a little confused in the morning until I felt Annie sleeping next to me, and everything came rushing back to me. I was supposed to go see London, but instead, I fucked someone else. A flash of guilt hit me for a second before I shook it off. That was not who I was, goddamn it. I saw by the clock on the dresser that it was almost seven which meant I could leave now and get home to shower before I had to go to the shop. I was supposed to meet with my car owner today about a new sponsor that wanted to sign on with me. Henry would be pleased.

I quietly slipped off the bed, making sure not to wake Annie, and went to find my clothes. They were right where I left them along with everything else on her living room floor. I dressed quickly and snuck out the door within ten minutes. I sprinted across the lawn to my car and jumped inside before I stuck the key inside the ignition. Again, I felt a little bit of guilt creeping up inside me at blowing London off last night, but it was something I had to do for myself and for her.

I drove home making sure to keep it around the speed limit and as I pulled into the parking lot of my apartment building, I felt a sense of relief wash over me. Unlike most of my fellow NASCAR drivers, I didn't feel the need to have a lavish home that I didn't really have a use for, instead keeping it simple with an upscale apartment. I didn't have a girlfriend, wife, or any pets to come home to so it didn't matter what the place really looked like although I *did* have someone come by and clean it up on Sunday's so that it didn't look too bad when I came home from a long race weekend.

I dumped my keys onto the table next to the door once I was inside my place before I made a beeline for the shower. I had about an hour before I had to get to the race shop, so I didn't have time to fuck around. The hot water felt great and I felt the rest of my hangover start to fade away as I washed up, wondering who the new sponsor might be. I had had the same sponsor for the past couple of years so it most likely would be a smaller one or a onetime deal, but I didn't want to be late for this meeting.

Chapter Four

London

After I realized that Mason actually wasn't going to show up like he said he was going to I ended up getting drunk on a cheap bottle of wine. Then, like the classy woman that I was, I passed out on the couch. If I had had his phone number, I would have texted him to never, *ever* talk to me again, but luckily for that bastard, I didn't. I should have known Mason was lying to me.

I woke up with the world's worst hangover on Brooklyn and Rand's couch and stared up at the ceiling, debating on whether I even wanted to get up this morning. Men were the absolute worst. I mean, they give you this amazing dick, but then they *were* the most amazing dicks. I knew Mason Pelletier was a liar, a fucking tease, and someone I should have stayed away from, but I had wanted him since the day I first met him.

I guess I got what I deserved.

I dragged my ass off the couch so I could rinse out my glass and ditch the wine bottle before Sully got home. I didn't want that hanging around, thanks. She and Rand had somehow gotten his doctor to let him leave for the hospital so they could have one night alone for their first night as husband and wife. I wasn't sure when she would be home, but I didn't want to look hungover even though I had a raging fucking headache that felt like my head might actually explode at any moment.

I climbed up the stairs to "my room" which really didn't feel like my room because it wasn't my house. It was Rand's house. Or rather, my sister and brother-in-law's house. Sure, he told me to make myself comfortable, decorate the room however I wanted, blah blah blah, but I didn't plan on living here for much longer. I wanted my own place now that school was over and needed to get a job, but who wanted to hire me? I was a musician and songwriter, but honestly? I didn't really think I was good at it. I guess that I could sort of sing, but also played the piano, and a few other instruments. What I really wanted to do was write songs, well country songs, but I would have to move to Nashville for that and I wasn't afraid to admit that scared the living shit out of me.

I stripped off my clothes before I climbed into the shower, making sure to stand underneath the water as long as humanly possible. I *did* love how I had my own bathroom here, and it was like a little slice of heaven. Back in Connecticut Sully and I had to share one shower, which at times could be hectic when we ended up needing it at the same time, but now I didn't have to worry about that. Once I was done washing off, I wrapped my hair in a towel and then ran my hand across the fogged-up mirror to stare at myself. It was a habit I couldn't seem to break even now.

I slowly ran my finger across the scars on my stomach as I remembered each one of them. The nights I had sat in my room back home trying to cut away everything I hated about myself. Recovery hadn't been easy, but I worked hard to stay on track. I would probably never love myself, but I had friends and family to support me. Who wouldn't let me get sick again.

I shook myself out of the daze I had entered before I whipped the towel off my head. I piled my hair back into a ponytail before I slathered on some pumpkin lotion left over from the fall and went back into the bedroom to find some clean clothes.

"Hello, little S." Mason grinned at me as he looked up from one of my notebooks I used to scribble down song ideas. I had left it and a few other things spread out on the small desk crammed into the corner. He slowly turned his body to face me and folded his arms across his massive chest.

I'm pretty sure I jumped ten feet at the sound of his voice. "What in the fuck? What are you doing here?" I exclaimed. "How did you get inside? You can't just break in."

Mason chuckled softly. "I didn't have to." He held out his hand to show me the keychain that dangled off his finger as he started toward me.

I took a couple of steps back to put some distance between us. "You need to leave, Pelletier." I pointed at the door. "Now."

"Why?"

"Why? You fucking blew me off last night, and what? You think you can just come here, and I'll just spread my legs for you? God only knows who or what you had wrapped around your dick last—"

Mason didn't let me finish my sentence as he closed the gap between us. He slammed his mouth against mine, his tongue slipping between my lips. I brought my hands up to slap at his chest before I changed my mind and clung to his shirt like my life depended on it while he pushed me back against the wall.

"You are like some drug that I can't seem to get enough of." He growled into my mouth. "I know that I shouldn't be here or have anything to do with you, but I can't seem to fucking stop myself. Tell me you don't feel the same." His espresso-colored eyes searched my face.

"I don't."

Mason's nostrils flared, but he didn't let go of me. "Liar, liar, pants on fire, baby." His lips brushed against mine when he spoke.

"Where were you last night? Hmm? You said you weren't going to fuck anyone else. Who's the liar now?" I slid my lips down to his chin.

"You know I'm not a one pussy type of guy," Mason reminded me as I licked his face lightly. "You know... fuck." He grunted when I bit down on his chin. His big hands came up to cup my cheeks. "What about you? What did you do last night?"

"You want to know what *I* did last night." I laughed bitterly. "I got drunk on cheap wine until I passed out on the couch, Mason." I pulled free of his hands. "Leave."

"London—"

"I want you to go before Sully shows up," I begged. "Because all that will do is bring on another whole heap of shit we both don't fucking need."

Mason planted both hands on the wall behind me to box me in as he searched my face. He looked confused, like maybe a woman had never told him no before. He moved closer and it took all I had not to grind against his impressive hard-on. We stared at one another for what seemed like forever until he finally spoke again.

"Where did you get those scars on your stomach?"

My eyebrows shot up so fast I thought they might fly right off my head. No one, not even Rush, had ever asked me that before. "It's none of your fucking business, Pelletier." My voice shook when I spoke. I hated how weak I sounded, and I hated that Mason was the one that made me feel like that.

Mason's hand suddenly gripped my jaw so tight it hurt. "Why don't you like to be touched unless it's fucking? What happened to you, London?" He tilted his head and I watched as his hair flopped down over his eyes.

I sucked in my breath when Mason pulled my bottom lip down with his thumb. I was still standing there completely naked and my nipples had become small pebbles pressed against his shirt. "It doesn't matter. None of it matters." I whimpered as Mason dropped his hand to wrap it around my throat just enough to apply a slight pressure.

"Why are you so damn stubborn?" He leaned closer like he was going to kiss me, but then we heard the sound of the garage door opening.

"You have to go," I wheezed. "That's Sully."

"I think it's a little too late to hide, baby." Mason's lips twitched into a smile. "She's already seen my car." He slid his lips against mine before he let go of me to take a step back. "This isn't over. You, me, this..." He waved his finger around in a circle between the two of us. "This entire fucking conversation, not by a long shot."

I watched as Mason walked out of my room like he did it every damn day. I quickly grabbed a pair of underwear with a matching bra before I slipped into clean boyfriend jeans and an oversize Juilliard sweatshirt before my sister caught me naked. I was halfway down the stairs when I heard hushed voices. I sank down onto the middle platform to eavesdrop on the conversation.

"It's none of your business, Mason. If she wanted to tell you or wanted you to know, you would know," Sully said.

I heard the sound of what might have been a fist hitting the counter. "Fuck that, Brooklyn, I deserve to know the truth."

"Why, because you slept together? London isn't your concern, Mason. She's mine to worry about."

"She's a grown-ass woman which means she isn't yours either. You try to shield her away from the rest of the world like she's some porcelain doll that might break, but she deserves so much better than that." Mason's voice had an edge to it I had never heard.

I couldn't help but smile at the way Mason defended me despite how he blew me off last night. No one had ever said something like that to or about me before. I moved down the next couple of stairs to try to see if I could hear them better and maybe catch a glimpse as well.

Brooklyn threw her hands up in the air. "Honestly, Mason? You couldn't handle my sister. She's wild, she's feral, and she's like nothing you've ever seen before." She shook her head as she looked out the window. "I'm not having this conversation with you."

Mason ran his hand through his hair. "Feral? Like an animal? What the fuck, Brooklyn. That's what I'm talking about when I say she deserves better. Are you only saying these things to me because of Coop?"

Shit, he didn't just go there.

Brooklyn spun around with fire in her eyes. "How *dare* you bring Cooper into this, Mason! You have no fucking clue what you're talking about. I want you to leave before I say something I shouldn't. I appreciate your concern about London, but she's better off without you in her life." She used quotes around the word concern like Mason didn't actually care about me. He did though.

Right?

"Fine," Mason spat back. "This isn't over."

"Trust me when I say this *is* over."

Mason slapped the palm of his hand on the counter before he marched out of the house, and I heard the door slam behind him. I looked back to see the key he had used to get inside sitting on the counter where his hand had hit. I wondered how long I should wait before I went downstairs, but I didn't have to worry.

"I didn't say anything," Brooklyn called to me. "You can come down now."

I slunk into the kitchen with my tail between my legs. "Thanks." I reached for the loaf of bread to make something to eat.

"Why, Lon? Why Mason of all the drivers—"

I placed two slices into the toaster before I met her eyes. They weren't angry, just concerned. I shrugged my shoulders. "I don't know." *Lie.* "I wish I had an answer for you, but I don't." Another lie.

Brooklyn walked around to get closer to me. "You don't love him, do you?" She scrunched her nose like she had just tasted something bitter.

"What? God, no." I grabbed one of the slices of toast as it popped out and bit into it so I wouldn't have to say anything else.

"You know I love you, right?" I nodded at my sister. "I'm only trying to protect you and the things that Mason said weren't true. He's a user, Lon. He isn't going to settle down."

I swallowed my bread. "Rand did." Shit, why did I say that?

"Rand is different." Brooklyn reached above her to take the peanut butter out of the cabinet. "Put this on there, please. You can't eat just plain toast." She held her hand out toward me. "Rand is different from any other man I've met. If you think Mason is going to change for you—"

"I don't nor would I want him to." I turned to face my sister. My wonderful, beautiful, fucking perfect sister. With her perfect fucking body, never ever frizzy hair and her amazing husband. She had a great fucking job, a fabulous son, and an even better best friend than I could ever dream of. "Just drop it, okay? You made your damn point." I grabbed the other piece of toast. "I'll be upstairs if you need me." I ignored the peanut butter and went back upstairs.

"London!"

I ignored Brooklyn, too, as I slammed my door shut and made sure to lock it behind me. I didn't want to deal with that shit now. I just wanted to be alone. Like always.

———

"Hey."

I looked up at the sound of Cooper's voice. "Brooklyn isn't here. She's out getting a dress for your party tonight." I went back to writing in my notebook. I had been writing songs lately or what I thought could be songs, but I didn't really think they were any good. It just felt good to get them out on paper instead of keeping them bottled up inside my head.

"I know." Cooper smiled at me and the look on his face just made my skin crawl. I wasn't sure what my sister saw in him. Sure, he was kind of cute with his rust-colored hair and emerald green eyes, but he was super creepy with the way he was always hitting on me when Sully wasn't paying attention. I wondered why he couldn't be more like his brother, Finn, who tried to talk to me about things I liked or enjoyed instead of trying to touch me. Or make me feel uncomfortable.

"Okay." I looked back down at my notebook, but my head shot back up when Cooper touched my arm.

"I was looking for you." His hand was still on my arm. "How are you? Sully said you hadn't been feeling that great lately."

I jerked away from his touch like it burned me. "I'm fine." I started to get to my feet, but Cooper stood in my way. I broke out into a faint sweat as I stared up at him.

"You're still a virgin, right?"

"That's none of your business," I whispered as I hugged my notebook tightly against my chest.

Cooper smirked. "Keep that cherry safe for me, little Sullivan." He ran the pad of his thumb against my cheek and I felt bile rise up in my throat.

"Hey man, are you ready to—" Mason stopped in the middle of his sentence. "Am I interrupting something?" Confusion was written on his handsome face.

"No." I was able to move away from Cooper and I bolted from the porch back into the house.

"Are you fucking stupid, Coop? Or are you trying to get yourself in trouble?" Mason exclaimed. "How old is that girl?"

Cooper laughed like it was nothing. "Relax, man. It's just harmless flirting. We do it all the time," he assured his friend.

"It didn't look that way from where I stood. She looked terrified."

"Whatever man, there are plenty of other girls out there," Cooper insisted.

I tried to hide in my bedroom that night instead of attending the party, but I couldn't. I tried to hide from Cooper, too, but he found me.

He ruined me that night.

Chapter Five

That conversation I had with Brooklyn didn't sit well with me, not to mention I immediately regretted leaving my spare key behind. Rand had given it to me years ago when he first had the place built and he said I could use it anytime I wanted.

Rand, not Brooklyn.

Alright, they were fucking married now, and I knew how he felt about her. But, having her treat London like that really pissed me the fuck off. London was an adult, not some child that needed her hand held like she was crossing a busy street. She held herself together better than most women I had slept with, not to mention she didn't take any shit from me. I couldn't figure out what the fuck Brooklyn's deal was.

I didn't have time to fucking go see Shepard at the hospital, but I knew he would understand. We had that kind of relationship. There was no sign of crazy-assed Annie when I pulled into my apartment complex and I could get ready to leave for the next race. I sent off a text as I was packing up my shit telling him to get his wife under control and as I dumped some clean clothes into my suitcase, I heard the phone ding back at me.

Shepard: *You can just fuck right off.*

I ground my teeth together. I knew he was just trying to get me going, but I also knew how he had to side with his wife. She was an important part of his life now, and I was actually proud of him for manning up like he did. I was not that guy nor would

I ever be when it came to women because I wanted to keep my balls intact. My phone went off again.

Shepard: *You need to figure out why you can't stay away from London and also stay the fuck away from her. Brooklyn isn't going to let you fuck her sister because it makes you feel good, dude.*

Was he kidding me right now? I resisted the urge to fling my phone across the room because one, they were expensive, and two, he was my best friend and telling me the truth. I answered his text with a question about why Brooklyn treated London the way she did. That left me wondering why I was suddenly so fucking curious about one woman. Again.

I slipped my phone into my pocket before I went into the kitchen to fix something to eat. I found some leftover pizza that didn't look *too* old and decided that would work. As I placed the box on the counter I felt my phone letting me know I had a text message.

Shepard: *Not for me to say, man. You'll have to ask London, which I'm betting you already fucking did.*

What was the big fucking secret? Honest to fucking Christ! Was she an alien or maybe a robot from that show *Westworld* or something else? I decided I wouldn't bother to text Rand back because that would only piss me off even more. Instead, I went to bed knowing I had a big weekend ahead of me.

Except, that didn't happen. I was lucky if I got maybe two or three solid hours of sleep. My dreams, if you could even call them dreams, were completely messed up. I dreamed that I was trying to rescue London like she was some sort of fucked-up princess trapped in a tower. Except instead of her hair that I had to climb, I had to fight off these monsters that looked like fucking brass keys with mouths that were full of needle teeth and one giant cyclops eye that bulged out of their heads.

I finally gave up sleeping around four in the morning, knowing it was useless to stay in bed any longer. I just hoped that it wasn't an indication of how the rest of my weekend was going to go. I needed this to be the best damn weekend I had in a long time with my new sponsor on board or I would never hear the end of it from Henry.

Walking into the garage on Friday afternoon and not having Shepard to hang around with was strange. It wasn't that I didn't have other friends in the sport, but he and I just always clicked. Sure, he was a few years younger than I was, but that never seemed to be an issue. Before he came along, it had just been me, Cooper Houston, and Lake Mills. Sometimes Eli, Rand's older brother, would hang around with us, but when I started racing he was already deep into his drug problems. Coop, Lake, and I were just three assholes hanging out, drinking too much, and picking up chicks.

"You look like shit." Lake elbowed me as I walked over to where he was standing. "Do I even want to ask what the fuck *you* did this weekend?"

"If your wife has already filled your head full of bullshit then you can fuck the hell off," I warned. Lake and I had been teammates since I started racing ten years ago. He had taken me under his wing, showed me the ropes and we had become fast friends. We had gotten into plenty of trouble together, but now that he was sober, married, and about to become a father he was different. It wasn't that I had a problem with that, but hanging out with him wasn't nearly as fun as it used to be.

Lake chuckled. "So, I guess it has a little something to do with London Sullivan?" He put his hand on my shoulder. "Brooklyn isn't exactly your biggest fan."

"Oh, and she's the president of *your* fucking fan club?"

Lake ran a hand through his blond hair. He was probably the only thirty-eight-year-old I knew that could pull off a ponytail and not look like a complete fucking tool. His green eyes darkened just before he spoke. "Look, we both know that Coop was a complete and total asshole to that woman. She didn't deserve all the shit he put her through and I'm sure we don't even know half of it, but for some reason, she's chosen to forgive me and overlook what happened—"

"Stop." I held up my hand as I made a gagging noise. "Enough you pussy-whipped bastard." I smirked at the way his eyes went wide. "I'm kidding, relax. I might have overstepped my bounds a little when I asked about London, but I don't understand why Brooklyn treats her like that." I scratched at the stubble on my face and realized I forgot to shave this weekend. Something flashed across his face that made me realize he knew something I didn't. "Spill it."

"No fucking way. Harper would kill me, and Sully would

never speak to me again. I can't have either of those things."

"Lake, you've known me longer than your wife. We've shared women together," I reminded him.

Lake looked around the crowded garage like Harper was going to pop out of a corner somewhere and scream "I knew it!" or something. "Keep your goddamn voice down, Pelletier. That was a long fucking time ago." He narrowed his eyes. "Someone hurt that girl so damn bad that she decided to hurt herself. She has some serious mental problems, dude. Why can't you just find someone normal to settle down with? I thought you and Apple were—"

"Apple is not my girlfriend, nor is she even close to being normal." Apple Birch was not the woman everyone thought she was. I had made a promise to a friend years ago and that was all she was to me. "Besides, who said I was looking to settle down?" I kid, trying to change the subject.

"So, you admit you have a thing for her? London, I mean?" Lake was never going to let that shit go.

"No." I shook my head as I saw Finn headed my way. Fucking Christ, what now? Was he going to give me shit about his precious fucking Brooklyn? We all knew how he felt about her, even now that she was married to Rand he still seemed to be madly in love with the woman. "I was curious and clearly I struck a few chords with big sis." I squared my shoulders as I prepared for my next battle. "Look, whatever it is you want to say, just don't." I cut Finn off before he had a chance.

Finn folded his arms across his chest. "I was only coming over to see how Shepard was." He looked between Lake and me.

"But, if I'm interrupting or whatever, I can go." His brows dipped slightly.

"He's fine. Same giant asshole as always." I assured him as I noticed the look Lake was giving me. He knew what I was thinking. Finn was not acting like normal since we weren't in the same crowd of friends. He never seemed to care much about Rand before, and they were teammates. "Who is driving his car while he's out?" Since Shepard's horrible crash that took him out of the rest of the season, we hadn't heard who would be the replacement driver.

Finn looked around the garage before he answered. "Watson Brooks." He shrugged. "Kids going places, you know, I mean Shepard invited him to the wedding so I guess he probably had a say in who got to drive his car, too." He suddenly pulled out his phone before he looked back up. "I'll be back." He disappeared as quickly as he appeared.

"That was fucking odd."

Lake smirked. "Harper thinks that he and Mia are fucking."

"Wait, what?" I exclaimed. "Mia? The cake decorator with the twins? Isn't she the one that just lost her husband?" I kind of fucked that one up when I showed up with Apple to the funeral, but I was trying to prove that there wasn't something going on with London. At the time there wasn't anything, but I had seen the way she was watching me.

"That's the one." Lake nodded as he pulled out his phone. "Apparently it started before that, but I can't be too sure." He brought his phone up to his ear. "Hey, freckles." He started to walk away from me to get a little privacy.

And just like that, I was the one who was alone. My best friend wouldn't be back at the track until next season, Lake was married with a kid on the way and Finn was fucking someone? How the hell did I end up the one alone? No, *fuck* that shit. After this practice session, I was going to either find a hot chick to hook up with or try to locate my usual pussy from Indy so that I wouldn't be spending the night by myself.

Sunday arrived faster than I thought it would. I loved race morning. The nerves, the anxiety, the roar of the fans as they started to fill up the seats and their excitement just radiated throughout the stands. I had the best damn fans, too.

Sure, we all said it, but mine *were* the fucking best. They were solid fucking people who never gave up on me even when I went six, eight, ten months without a win and I always said when I won that it was for them. Yes, I made sure to include my sponsors, my owner in there, but my fans were the reason I was able to keep doing my job. If I didn't have people rooting for me every week or buying my merchandise, I wouldn't be able to do what I did. I wouldn't be here right now.

After our mandatory driver meeting, I always made sure to sneak in some time for autographs. I tried to locate the kids first because they always had the best reaction. My mother took me to one NASCAR race when she was alive and I was lucky enough to meet my favorite driver. I still have the picture she took of us together hanging up in my apartment because it meant so much to me. It was such a huge deal that I wanted to make someone else feel the way I did and maybe he or she would end up being a driver someday.

Then it was off to win today's race. Hey, I had to think positive about it, right?

I ran my hand through my hair wondering if it was time to get a haircut when I got home, when I saw Lake grinning like a total asshole as he stood next to his car. At some point between last night and this morning Harper had shown up and he had his arm locked around her waist like he was afraid she might make a break for it or possibly someone might try to steal her away. Again, I swore to myself I wouldn't be that kind of guy that I would forever remain a bachelor until the day they buried me in the ground. My usual girl, Missy, had been more than happy for me to come visit her last night since I think she thought I had forgotten her or something.

I tried really hard to bust a nut, but just like with Annie, my cock wasn't having it. I was able to get hard, but after that? Nada. Missy tried her best to get me off, but no matter what she did, it didn't work. I told her it was just nerves and she seemed to believe me, but something in her eyes told me she didn't. It knew that it wasn't fucking nerves. It was fucking London Sullivan.

Harper smiled at me as I approached. "Hello, Mason." Her voice sounded normal, but her gray eyes told me she knew about the argument I had with her best friend. Awesome.

"Hello, Harper, how are you feeling?" I asked politely as I

glanced at my teammate.

Harper placed a hand over her small bump. "I'm good, Mason, thank you." She leaned against Lake as her eyes told me not to go there with her. Fucking chicks, man.

"Well, that's great." I hated small fucking talk. "Good luck, man." I jutted my chin at her husband before I hurried on my way.

Today felt good. Really fucking good, and I needed that. I needed a win more than I needed breathe in my lungs.

<u>Chapter Six</u>

London

I blew the smoke from my cancer stick out the window before I crushed it out in the ashtray. I kept the window open to air out the smell because Sully would freak if she knew I was smoking and twirled the keychain around my finger, just watching it spin around. It was the same one that Mason had left on the counter just a couple of days ago, and I had snagged it when Brooklyn hadn't been looking. The actual keychain itself was in the shape of the state of California which was the state he was born in and it made me wonder if he ever went back there. For races probably, but did he have family there? I knew from reading his biography that his mother passed away when he was a teenager, but what about anyone else? His dad? Grandparents? Fuck, why did I even give a shit anyway?

I slipped the key back into my pocket before I reached for the candy apple body spray on the bookshelf and sprayed it to try to dissipate the rest of the smoke smell that filled the room as well as my clothes and skin. For some reason, I liked having the key near me. Like having a part of Mason near me or something stupid like that.

I had holed myself up in my room for the past couple of days, only coming out to eat. I was still pissed at my sister, but I wasn't even sure why now at this point. She had left the house this morning to go to the hospital where Rand ended up after his accident so that she could help him get discharged and bring him back home. They were going to spend a few days together before they came back, so that left me alone in the house. Luckily, Sully had decided to take RJ, too. Not that I didn't love the kid or anything because he was the coolest nephew on the planet, but I was glad to have the entire house to myself. I just wasn't sure what I was going to do with myself.

I stomped down the stairs with my phone in my hand and suddenly I had a great idea. It was Friday morning... what if I threw a party and invited Rush and maybe a few of my other ED friends to come down? I mean, Rand had told me to make myself at home in his giant fucking house. This place just screamed throw a party and there was so much room inside as well as out for people to hang.

I quickly shot off a group text asking everyone to come down along with the address. Of course my bestie was the first one to respond.

Rush: *Are you fucking KIDDING, Lon? I'm packing my shit and on my way. Bitch, you better be ready for the party of the year.*

I chuckled to myself as I opened the cabinets to check for booze. Of course my sweet sister and dear old bro-in-law wouldn't have anything or maybe they did, but just hid it because of me. That was most likely the case since Brooklyn didn't trust me as far as she could fucking throw me. Looked like I was going to be running out to get some alcohol for this thing and maybe a few other things, too, while I was at it. Another text came in as I was trying to decide which car I should take to the store.

Nola: *I'm already on my way. We're fucking shit up.*

I tucked my phone back into my back pocket and then put my hands on my hips to look at my choice of vehicles. Nothing too fancy which actually surprised me. No Tesla, Lamborghini, or Ferrari for Rand Shepard. Parked in the five-stall garage, minus the Jeep I watched Sully drive off in, was a Ford SUV, Sully's Ford Focus and a motorcycle. Bummer I couldn't take out some expensive shit, but I guess I would take the Focus since I hoped that wouldn't get me in too much trouble. Not that I cared, but I should probably stay on the down low. I hit the button to open the garage door before I slipped into the car.

I drove for a bit, blasting the local country music station until I found a shopping center that happened to have both a grocery store and package store. I figured I could hit up some sort of party place tomorrow before everyone showed up to maybe spruce up the place a bit and *really* turn it into a fucking party. I found a parking spot before I grabbed my purse to hurry inside.

The bell on the door of the store rang my entrance and it was like walking into heaven. The sound of the violin and banjo filled the air as the twangy voice of Luke Combs flowed through my ears. Of course in North Carolina they would have country playing in their liquor stores. We didn't have anything like that back home. Maybe I should stop thinking about it as home since I didn't think that I was ever going back there.

"Good afternoon. Do you need help with anything?"

I hadn't even noticed the pretty silver-haired girl behind the counter. I flashed a quick smile. "Well, I'm having a party tomorrow night and I need to get some good stuff. It's not a lot of people, but I want to make sure I have enough. I love your hair, by the way. I always wanted to do that to mine, but I doubt that I could pull it off. You know with my dark hair and how hard it would be just to bleach it, never mind the upkeep." I was nervous and I had started to babble.

Her lips turned into a giant smile. "I'm Tessa Flowers," she introduced herself. "You know, my friend Jean works at a salon." She tucked a loose piece of her own hair behind her ear. "She could totally color yours, I mean, if you wanted. Not that you don't have great hair because, girl, you fucking do." Tessa came out from behind the counter. She was thin, but not too thin and a couple inches taller than my five foot two. Dressed in a pair of black leggings and a tattered Keith Urban T-shirt that hung off her shoulder, I instantly liked her.

"Maybe." I chewed on my lip. "I'm London Sullivan." I realized I hadn't told her my name.

"On vacation?" Tessa asked. "I only ask because you don't have an accent from here. Not that it's any of my business," she added. "I don't want to overstep my bounds."

I shook my head. "No, my sister just got married and we moved here—" I stopped myself before I went any further. I didn't want to tell Tessa who Sully married because it was a NASCAR nation down here. "I just invited a bunch of my friends to come visit while my sister and brother-in-law are gone."

"Cool."

A thought occurred to me. "Do you want to come? To the party, I mean? I don't have any friends here besides my sister and her new husband. You could bring a friend or whatever, too." I didn't want to sound too needy, but I was kind of desperate.

"Why don't you give me your digits and then I can get your address? I don't have any plans for tomorrow." Tessa had her cell phone in her hand. "Plus, if you need anything else or whatever I can bring that." Tessa added my number as I rattled it off to her.

We made small talk for a little bit longer before Tessa promised to text me and I left. I felt a little happier and it felt like I had a little bit more of a bounce in my step as I headed back to my car.

———————

Rush Showed up at the house around eleven a.m. the next morning. I was so excited to see him that I nearly knocked him over when I hugged him, and I think that surprised both of us. He looked good, too, better than the last time I saw him, and that meant he must have been taking really good care of himself.

"You look fucking gorgeous." Rush kissed my cheek once I let go of him. Tall, blond and beautiful, Rush was probably every girl's dream except he was more into boys than girls. Which was fine because it made it much easier for me to trust him the way I did.

I rolled my eyes. "Stop." I swatted at him. "What about you? You must have a new guy in your life." I watched the color appear in his cheeks. "Why haven't you told me? Rush, you're supposed to be my best friend!"

"It's nothing, Lon." His eyes were wide as he looked around the house. "Jesus, look at this fucking place." Rush muttered.

"Don't avoid the question, Rush."

A sly smile appeared on my best friend's face. "All I'm going to tell you is that his name is Brad. Happy?" Rush's eyes danced with happiness. "Show me around this freaking mansion because I have never been inside a house this big."

I knew that when Rush changed the subject that would be the end of the conversation. He would tell me about Brad if and when he was ready. That was just how he was about his private life. We made our way around the house which wasn't a mansion, but since Rush grew up in an apartment and still lived in one, I knew why he would feel that way. The house was a bit overwhelming and I would never feel like it was my home. We ended up upstairs in my room, where Rush nodded his approval.

"This is amazing, London." He peeked through one of my songbooks. "You really should have someone, although I don't know who, read this. You're so damn good." He beamed at me. "What's going on with you?" Rush could always read me so well. That's why we were so close.

"I'm fine." *Lie.*

Rush's eyebrows shot up. "That so?" he asked as he moved closer. "It wouldn't have anything to do with a certain driver that you were after for so many years and now that you've had him?" He made a heart with both of his hands by placing his index fingers and thumb together.

"Stop it!" I put both of my hands on Rush's wrists to push them down. "I'm kind of lonely here. It's not my home and I just... I don't know." I sighed softly as I looked up at him. "Why don't we start getting this place ready for the party?" I suggested. It looked like neither one of us wanted to talk about our love lives right now.

Rush agreed and before long we had the country music blasting while we decorated with some of the things I had picked up. We ordered a couple of pizzas to be delivered later and once we both had showered and dressed, we were ready for the party to begin.

I decided to dress casual, but not too casual in a minidress with a scoop neck and wide cut-outs around the shoulder. It had a cut paisley print and since my boobs were pretty much nonexistent, I didn't bother with a bra, just a pair of paisley colored panties.

Nola showed up around the time I had just finished getting dressed. Nola, or should I say Penelope Pagan, was the first girl I met when I went to Washington DC when Sully and Rand sent me to the last clinic. She was the bright star that I needed in my life, the loud, obnoxious friend that I had been missing and we bonded instantly. With her bright red hair and green eyes, she was hard to miss whenever we went out.

"This house is intense." Nola didn't try to hug me. She knew how I was about that. "Your sister lucked out in the man department, huh?" Her British accent was faint since she had been living in the US for nearly twenty years. It only came out when she was mad or on certain words. "Rush, get over here!"

She hugged him happily as I noticed another car pull up the driveway.

"O-M-G!" Tessa exclaimed when she saw me before she threw her arms around me. I stiffened at the unwelcomed contact and wished I had thought to tell her about the no touching thing. It wasn't something I could easily bring up in conversation via text though and we really hadn't texted too much since we met. She pulled back to look at me. "You are so damn adorable. Where did you get this dress? I could never fucking pull it off, but shit, you are rocking it." She giggled happily.

Tessa was dressed in a red lace dress that was off the shoulders with three-quarter length sleeves that fell to her knees. "You are kidding, right?" I raised my eyebrows.

"This is Jean Costa." Tessa placed her hand on the dark-haired girl dressed in black leather pants and a plain white tee that had climbed out of the passenger side of her car.

"It's nice to meet you." Jean nodded at me.

When we went back inside the house Rush had mixed a few drinks for everyone and that was when the party finally felt like a party. With a glass in my hand and booze in my veins, I felt like I could finally loosen up a bit. Relax, have a good time. Make some much-needed friends with the locals.

Tessa told me she had been working at the package store for a couple of years, but also had a job working at a motel. "It's a dump, but I can live there for free," she added as she drained her glass.

"So, you're not from around here?" I asked as we went into

the kitchen to get another drink.

Tessa chewed her lip as she avoided making eye contact. "Um, no. I moved here to try to get a new start." She shrugged. "I didn't plan on working two jobs to have to do that, but it's not *that* bad. I met you, right?" Tessa leaned a hip against the counter. "You're only the second friend I've made since I got here, and Jean doesn't really count since she's my hairdresser."

"So." I wiggled my eyebrows at her as a thought suddenly entered my head. "Do you think that your friend Jean could do something with my hair?"

Tessa threw her head back and laughed. "Shit, that's what I'm talking about." She hooked her arm through mine. "This is going to be *so* much fun."

<u>Chapter Seven</u>

MASON

I'm pretty sure that I just walked into a warzone. There was no other way to describe the scene that was happening before my eyes. After the amazing fucking race yesterday, I won in case you were wondering; I got back to my RV to realize I had a text from Shepard telling me he was on his way home. That just added to my happiness and so when I got home, rested a bit, and showered, I decided to come visit my friend.

I just didn't expect to walk into this... this nightmare that I was watching unfold.

From what I could tell, London must have thrown a party while her sister was gone. Obviously not the best idea, but given the circumstances, I don't blame her. The place was completely fucking trashed and—who the fuck was *that* guy? The tall blond that I saw in the corner with the redhead?

"You told me that I should make myself at home!" London exclaimed as she got right in her sister's face. "You said I should make this place my home, you told me that! That's what I was doing!" She threw her hands up in the air. What in the hell of all things holy did she do to her hair? It was bleached white.

Brooklyn looked like she was going to blow her stack. "I didn't say throw a fucking party with your friends, London. We never said that was how you could make yourself comfortable, we thought you'd unpack a few boxes." She closed her eyes like she was trying to control herself.

That must be Rush, the best friend. I didn't like the fucker the second I laid eyes on him and I wanted him gone, NOW! I narrowed my eyes as I watched him, but he was too busy talking to the redhead and now some gray-haired girl. Who *were* these people?

London's face twisted into confusion. "So, what? I'm supposed to just hide up in my room like some deranged fucking princess and wait for my prince to save me? I've got some news for you, that isn't going to happen. I'm not you, Sully. I don't get to have the perfect life with the kid or the husband and any of that shit. Not now or ever!" I swung my head back around at London's words. It was like she had been inside my dream or something. "I can't fucking do this!" she screamed before she threw her hands up in the air and headed toward the front door.

I wasn't even aware that I had followed London outside until I was outside. She had her arms wrapped around herself, and it killed me to see her like that. "What did you do to your hair, little Sullivan?" I blurted out before I could stop myself.

London spun around to face me. "I don't have time for your games, Pelletier. I can't—" She closed her eyes while she tried to get herself together. "I can't live here with them. They tell me to make myself at home, enjoy myself, and when I do? They fucking scream and yell at me like a child. RJ is a child!" Her eyes glistened with tears. "I won't stay here. I won't—"

"Easy." I touched her cheek with my hand and used my knuckles to turn her face up to look at me.

"Mason, I'm fucking serious. I'm going back to Connecticut."

I didn't fight London as she pushed away from me. "Where, though? Your family is here. Harper is here. Finn is here." I pinched my lips together tightly before I spoke again. "I'm here." My voice sounded so different.

London stared up at me. That dress, shit, it was perfect and fit her in all the right places. "You're not my family," she whispered. "You're just a guy that wants to stick his dick inside me and get off." She sniffed as the tears that filled her eyes slipped down her cheek. "I'll find a place back there. I can get a job. I'll be fine." She crossed her arms across her chest. "I won't stay here anymore."

"Stay with me."

"What?"

I couldn't believe I said those words either. Me, the guy who had never let a woman sleep at his house or in his bed, just invited a girl he barely knew to stay with him. "Just, you know, until you can find somewhere here. You want to stay close to RJ and your sister. Brooklyn loves you, you know that. She's just trying to take care of you."

"She embarrassed me in front of all of my friends," London reminded me. "I can't stay with you, Mason."

"It's fine. I have plenty of room." I lived in a one-bedroom apartment, but hey, whatever.

London dragged her teeth across her bottom lip. "I need to get a couple of things before I leave."

"If it's clothes—"

"I need a few things, Mason." London shook her head. "Just wait here." She hurried back into the house and I realized what I had just done. I had invited the one girl that I couldn't seem to stop thinking about to come live in my fucking apartment.

"ARE YOU FUCKING KIDDING?" Brooklyn's shrill voice interrupted my thoughts. "Go home, Mason! Leave my sister the fuck alone. You have no idea what you're getting yourself into."

I squared my shoulders as I turned around. "Look, Brooklyn, I know you're upset and worried, but—"

"Worried? Fucking Christ, that isn't even close to how I feel." Brooklyn shook her head as she pointed a finger toward the house. "That girl is a ticking fucking time bomb. You think a party upset me? Mason, she's done so much worse. In and out of hospitals since she was thirteen, suicide attempts, cutting." She stopped, and I watched the color as it drained from her face when she realized how far she had gone. "You can't handle London, but I can. Please, just leave now and I'll handle this just like I always do."

London came down the walkway with a bag in her hands. I watched her eyes flash angrily at her sister before she turned to me. "I'm going to be at Mason's. Rand has the number if you need me." She headed straight to my car.

"I can handle this," I assured her.

"But, you can't." Brooklyn touched my wrist. "Trust me, Mason, I'm not doing this or saying this to be the fucking bad guy here. She is *Chernobyl* waiting to explode."

"I said I could handle it and I meant I will fucking handle it." I pushed her hand away. "I'll call you or Rand if we need anything." But as I walked to my car, I wondered if I could. Everything that Brooklyn said rang in my ears. I might have just bit off more than I could chew.

London didn't say a single word single word on the quick ride back to my place. I wasn't too surprised. She had been upset and I'm sure she was exhausted now. I pulled into the apartment complex and parked my car before I glanced her way.

"You live here?"

"Sorry it's not Buckingham Palace," I teased. That hair was terrible and I was going to get it fixed for her. I didn't care what she thought.

A smile tugged at her pouty lips. "No, I mean, you don't have some giant fucking house filled with rooms you never use? Cars you don't drive?" London's blue eyes were curious as she searched my face.

"Oh, like Rand? Is that it? Well..." I started to climb out of the car. "I don't really need all that. I'm not home that much and when I am, I don't need some big house that is going to take up space for someone else."

London followed slowly behind me as she clutched her bag to her chest. "Rand's house just needs some work," she whispered like she was defending him all of a sudden.

I stopped to unlock the door before I turned to look down at her. "I'm not knocking the guy. He had a rough childhood. I get why he wants shiny stuff and a big house. Brooklyn and RJ make it a home." I flipped the light. "After you." I stood back so London could step inside.

She looked around the small living room. "This is nice, too." She smiled up at me. "Look, I can go stay with Rush," she suggested.

"No."

London's lips parted slightly. "Can I tell you a secret?" The way she was looking at me right now made my cock come alive and all I could think about was ripping that dress off her tiny body and fucking her into next Sunday. "Rush is gay." She smirked at me before she sat down on the couch. "I'll sleep here." She patted the cushion next to her.

"You're sleeping in my room, little Sullivan." I watched her cringe when I called her that. Was it always that way or just now? Did I call her that because Cooper did? "It's this way." I pointed toward the hallway so that she would get up. London stood up again and followed me without saying a word. "The shower is connected to this room, but there is a half bath down the hall," I told her. "If you're hungry, there should be some fresh food in the kitchen which is back through the living room."

"Thank you."

"Of course," I said softly. "If you need anything, just come find me." I disappeared back into the living room so that I could give her some privacy.

My phone had been going crazy and I could only imagine who it was. Rand, Finn, some unknown number that I assumed was Brooklyn, and Lake. All of them were blowing up my phone with texts. I didn't have time for them right now. I needed to figure out what I was going to do with London Sullivan in my bedroom and how I was going to handle this. I decided the best thing to do was sleep on it first and deal with it in the morning.

———————

"You're kidding." Apple's blue eyes were wide as she stared at me. She was the first person I could think of that would help me, and she didn't even ask. Just jumped in her car and headed over without even batting an eye.

I looked at her over the top of my coffee cup. "She's in my room." I placed my hand over hers before she got up. "She needs clothes and I don't know anything about that. Can you take her shopping?"

Apple had shown up at my house fifteen minutes after I called her. Face full of makeup, blonde hair pulled back in a high ponytail, wearing jeans that looked painted on and a crop top that left little to the imagination. I don't think I had ever seen her at a loss for words, but right now she sat there staring at me with her mouth hanging slightly open.

I turned to look down at Frankie, Apple's daughter, who was lying on the floor coloring and in her own little world. She had big green eyes and curly auburn hair that matched her father's, and I adored her to pieces. I had promised her father that I would take care of both of them if something happened and I did my best, but sometimes it was hard when Apple would only let me help with Frankie. I offered to move them into a nicer apartment, get her a better car, anything she wanted, but Apple wouldn't hear of it.

"Mason?" London was suddenly standing there with her hair, which sweet baby Jesus I was going to get taken care of *today*, a mess from sleep and confusion was written all over her face. She had found one of my shirts decked out with my sponsor on it and it was so big it fell past her knees. Just seeing London dressed in my clothes made my fucking dick twitch inside my jeans as I soaked it all in. She took one look at Apple, Frankie and then me before her blue eyes turned to steel. "I'm interrupting." She started to back up.

I was on my feet so fast I nearly knocked over the coffee table. "It's not what you think, baby," I assured her, but she twisted under my arm and rushed down the hallway. I hardly had time to make it into the bedroom before London turned to smack me in the chest. "She's my friend, little Sullivan."

"Bullshit," London hissed and pushed at my hands as I tried to hold her against me. "I know who she is and I know *what* she did. How could you invite her here?" She couldn't get away from me this time. I had her boxed in against the dresser. "Let me go, Mason," she warned.

"Apple is my friend, London. That's all she is to me. What you think happened between her and Rand? Never fucking happened."

"You're a liar," London seethed. "I don't believe you and I don't want to stay here anymore."

My lips landed against London's before I could stop them. I needed to taste her, breathe her in and I couldn't deny myself that anymore. The whimper that escaped her mouth was all I needed to hear to drop my hand down to her ass so that I could palm it while our tongues slicked and slid together. Fuck, what was the deal with this fucking girl? I couldn't seem to stop myself no matter what and all I wanted to do right now was sink my cock so far inside her pussy that she screamed my name.

"Stop, please fucking stop," London begged as I pressed myself further against her. "I can't... no." Her hands came up to my chest.

The way her voice sounded made me take a step back. "Little Sullivan—"

"Don't you fucking call me that!" she exclaimed before she buried her face into the palms of her hands and crumpled to the floor.

Fuck.

I dropped down next to London as she wept. I wasn't good at this, shit, I didn't know how to handle it at all. I soothed her hair back on her head and gently rubbed London's back until she finally looked up at me with red eyes and tear-stained cheeks. "I hate that nickname." Her voice was so quiet I could barely hear her. "London is fine. Lon, anything but *that*." She didn't even say it herself.

"Understood." I kept rubbing her back.

London sighed before she leaned into me. "She's really just your friend? Apple, I mean?" She sniffed softly. "I mean, that's obviously not your kid because she looks too much like..." She sat back to look at me with wide eyes. "No." She shook her head.

Shit, this was not for me to say. It was obvious to me or really anyone that knew him, that Cooper Houston was Frankie's father. London wasn't stupid. She knew it, too. "You have to be careful about this." I urged. "No one knows about Frankie."

"That bastard raped—" She stopped and clapped her hand over her mouth and dropped her eyes to the floor.

Did London just say what I think she did? I let my hand move up to her cheek before I gripped her jaw. "You do not get to stop talking, London." Her eyes were wide with fright. "Finish that damn sentence." She shook her head. "I swear to fucking God." I gritted my teeth together.

"I can't."

I let go of London. "Get dressed," I instructed her. "You're going shopping with Apple and you're doing something with that fucking hair. Don't even fight me on that." I wouldn't let her interrupt me. I slammed the door hard enough behind me when I left the bedroom, I swear the whole apartment shook.

―――――――

This was supposed to be Cooper's party, but I couldn't seem to find the fucker anywhere. At first I figured that he had slipped away with Brooklyn, but she was standing in the other room talking to Finn and some big-chested redhead I had never met before.

I left the raging party and headed outside to find my friend, wondering why he didn't just do what I did and let chicks know he wasn't a one-woman type of guy. He already had two chicks that didn't know about one another, and I knew it was a recipe for fucking disaster. I guess when you're the golden boy of NASCAR you have to keep up an image, but the one he'd been showing me lately wasn't pretty. I was pretty sure he'd knocked up the girl in North Carolina, told her he would marry her and then put a fucking ring on Brooklyn's finger. There was no way he was going to keep his image clean when word got out about that.

I was coming around the side of the house when I saw him and it was obvious he wasn't alone. Shit, was he fucking someone else at his fucking fiancée's house? Coop really did have big fucking balls.

"Let me go."

"Relax, little Sullivan, you know you want this." Cooper's voice slurred when he spoke. "You've always wanted it."

Was he seriously chasing after the little sister again? I didn't think that girl was even legal. He was going to get his dick chopped off and handed to him if he kept this nonsense up. As I drew closer to them in the moonlight, I saw the tears on her cheeks.

"Please, I already told you I wouldn't tell Sully."

Cooper grunted and I heard the tear of fabric as he pulled on her dress. "I know how much you love your big sister, London. I'm not worried about you opening that pretty little mouth of yours." His hand wrapped around her neck. "Unless it's to suck my cock."

"Cooper!" I spat out his name. "What the fuck are you doing?"

My supposed friend spun around at the sound of my voice, but when he saw it was just me, he relaxed. At least he let go of

London. "You want some, too?" Cooper chuckled like what he said was actually funny. "Little Sullivan isn't a virgin anymore, but that little pussy is super fucking tight." He grinned as he turned back to face the girl again. "Isn't that right?" His hand came up to stroke her cheek and she recoiled at his touch.

London was absolutely fucking terrified of Cooper. Did he rape her?

As she began to cry again, I realized what a horrible person my friend was and how badly I wanted to punch him. "Sure, right." I pushed Cooper out of the way. As I leaned down, I pressed my lips against her ear. "Relax, baby, I'm not going to hurt you," I assured her before I glanced over my shoulder to look at Coop, only to find that he had slumped down against the tree and was passed out. What a fucking dick.

London grabbed my arms. "Please, Mason, I should just go—"

"Easy, I got you." I scooped up her small frame into my arms and was surprised when she clung to me like a child. "Tell me which one is your room and I'll get you there without anyone even noticing." Her eyes were big and blue as she stared at me.

London nodded. "Up the stairs, to the right. It's the first door. You can't miss it." She buried her face against my neck as I began to walk.

Not a single person was even watching as I slipped back inside the house and I was able to quickly get up the stairs two at a time without worry. I kicked the door shut behind me before I placed London on the bed. "Baby, you should talk to someone about what happened. About what Coop did to you." Her little chest moved fast as she tried to catch her breath. "Hey." I sat down next to her thinking she might freak out, but instead she blinked those baby blues at me and it had my head hurting something terrible.

London shook her head so hard her ponytail slapped her in the face. This girl was beautiful, fragile, and broken in pieces all because of my supposed friend. "Please, Mason, I can't do that to my sister." She reached for my hand with her two small ones and they were like ice. "Sully loves him so much...I..." Tears filled those eyes again and my heart nearly burst from my chest.

"Brooklyn would never stay with him if she knew what he did to you, London." I pointed out as she released my hand. "Wouldn't you rather she do that?" I looked around the room for a second to take in the country musician posters, the keyboard in the corner, and the NASCAR memorabilia that was scattered around the room.

London touched my arm. "I can't do that to my sister," she whispered and her eyes widened when I stood up. "Do you... could you stay here? Just until I fall asleep?" A blush appeared on her cheeks as she spoke.

I nodded.

"Mason, can you promise me you won't tell anyone about what happened tonight? What you saw and what Cooper did?"

"That's not a promise I want to keep."

"Please." Those fucking blue eyes again. It was wrong for me to think London Sullivan was so fucking beautiful, right? I stuck out my pinky and a smile tugged at her plump lips.

We made a promise that night to never tell a soul about what happened.

Cooper died two weeks later leaving behind a pregnant girlfriend, a heartbroken fiancée, an angry best friend, a legion of devastated fans, and an innocent girl he ruined. Forever.

And I simply locked it away inside my brain until right this very second.

<u>Chapter Eight</u>

London

I couldn't believe that Mason expected me to actually go anywhere near that fucking woman. Not after she tried to break up Rand and Sully. He had some seriously big balls if he thought that was going to happen. And she had a daughter! With fucking Cooper Houston, of all people.

Cooper not only ruined my life, but had a fucking kid with someone else. Someone else who obviously had it out for Brooklyn, and I had to tell her. Why was it some big damn secret? My sister deserved to know the truth about him especially now. Except, there was more to that secret then just a love child.

I chewed on my fingernail while I tried to figure out how to get out of this. I could go in there and tell them both to go screw themselves. Or, I could just tell Apple, seriously her name was Apple, which I would burn in hell before I would be alone in a car with her.

"London?" There was a knock at the door.

"Go the fuck away," I spat back. "I have nothing to say to you."

The door opened anyway. Guess she doesn't understand English either. I folded my arms across my chest as I stared her down. Apple had on too much makeup; her jeans were so tight I swear I could read her lips and that top she had on looked ready to burst apart so that you could see her fucking tits. Super classy, Mom.

"Look—"

I shook my head. "No, you don't get to talk." I jumped up and Mason's shirt fell to my knees. "You ruined my sister's life. Before and after Cooper." I hated saying his name out loud. "Why? Why do you hate her so much?"

Apple pressed her lips together. "There's a lot you don't know," she whispered. "I don't think now is the time to talk about that. My daughter is in the other room and even though she knows who her daddy was, she doesn't know much about him."

I laughed bitterly. "Lucky for her."

"You're upset."

"You fucking think?" I snapped back. "You don't know anything about me. I'd like to keep it that way. We're not going to be friends, not now or ever."

Apple let out a heavy sigh before she turned to leave the room. "If it makes any difference, I didn't know about Brooklyn until after he died. Coop had already promised me the world and I was already pregnant." She stopped at the door. "Then he died and left us alone. I didn't follow racing so I had no idea that he had a fiancée back in Connecticut that he was hiding from me and she didn't know that he was hiding me down here." Apple glanced over her shoulder at me. "I was jealous, and what I did was wrong when I tried to break them up. I'm sorry that I did that. It was childish, stupid, and mean." She quietly closed the door behind her.

I was stunned, to say the least. I knew what a creep Cooper was, but Sully? She didn't find out until much later. I never told her what he did to me, and I wondered if he had more than just Apple hidden away. What if he had more girlfriends? More kids? I shuddered at the thought.

I quickly changed out of Mason's shirt and put back on the dress I was wearing last night when he brought me here. Then I brushed out my hair, which looked fucking terrible without any color in it, and pulled it up in a messy bun before I stuffed my phone into my bra. I wasn't about to go anywhere with that woman, no matter what Mason said to me.

I pulled the curtain back. I loved that this was the first floor. I didn't have to worry about falling or breaking anything. I had escaped from much, much worse when I was a kid. The first hospital that Sully had me stay at I left after two days and I just climbed out the window, down a tree that was next to it and broke my ankle. I didn't care. I needed out. So this was nothing compared to that.

I pushed the window open, then the screen before I slipped outside feet first. I made sure to close them both behind me before I started to walk away from the building. I wasn't sure where I was going. I had no money, no vehicle, and honestly? I felt like I had no friends. Sully had totally embarrassed me last night so if I had had the chance to make new ones last night that was totally gone now.

"Are you kidding me right now, London?" I felt a hand grip my arm and spin me around. "You didn't have to climb out the fucking window," Mason hissed.

"I'm not going shopping with her."

Mason let out a huff. "So, you thought the easy way out was

to climb out my window instead of talking to me like an adult?"

"I tried to do that and you told me I was going. I get that you want me to get clothes or think I need my hair done. Fine, but I'll go alone or with you. But not with her."

"Apple."

"I don't fucking care what her name is!" I exclaimed and watched his eyebrows shoot up.

Mason tugged on my arm. "Please, come back to my apartment. I'll have Apple leave. Will that make you feel better?" His eyes had grown soft.

"I don't believe you." I glared at him.

"London." Mason's nostrils flared. "You need to come inside." He was fighting to control himself now.

I had a way of pushing people. I had done it with Brooklyn so many times. Our grandparents, too. I hadn't spoken to them in so long now because they had basically given up on me. I let a slow smile creep across my face as I moved closer. "Are you going to spank me, Mason?" White heat flared between my legs at the thought of his hands on me. It was just like me to go from one extreme to the next. "Is that what you're going to do if I don't behave like a good little girl?"

"Don't test me, baby." There was warning in his voice, but something else, too.

"So, naughty," I cooed softly while I slowly ran my hands palm first up his chest.

"Fucking hell, London." Mason gritted his teeth. "How can you... I'm taking you back to the apartment." He brought his lips down to mine. Close enough to kiss me, but he didn't. "Am I clear?"

"Crystal."

I followed him back to the apartment and was surprised to see that there was no sign of Apple or her kid. It was like they had never been there at all. Mason had gone into the kitchen, so I went in to find him. I gasped when he suddenly had me pinned against the wall.

"What have you done, London? Why do you insist on driving me crazy?" The pads of his fingers danced against my cheek as he grabbed my hair into a tight ponytail and tugged it so I had to look up at him. I'd be a liar if I said my pussy didn't automatically start to ache with need.

I opened my mouth to object, to fight him, to do something, but Mason's seared to mine before I had the chance. Instead, I heard myself moan as his tongue slipped between my lips to flirt with my own while he made sure to grind his hard, thick cock against me.

"We can't keep doing this, Mason," I murmured as I let him pick me up so that I could wrap my legs around his waist.

Mason's lips never left mine as his hands tugged my panties down my legs and unbuckled his pants. "What are we doing, baby?" His eyes smoldered with fire when I met them.

I couldn't think now. Not with Mason's cock so close to being inside me. "Fuck me," I begged him. I nearly came when he slammed me back against the wall and he slipped himself inside me without a second thought. His dick would never *not* make me feel amazing. I felt my eyes roll back slightly as Mason pulled back just to do it again. And, again. I cried out with pleasure as I felt myself already fighting my climax.

"That's what you wanted, isn't it?" Mason's hand gripped my hip so tight I was sure it would leave a mark. "Look at me, London," he instructed me. "I want to see your face when you come all over my cock."

I whimpered when I saw the look in his eyes. The heat that drove me so fucking crazy that I hated myself for it. But at the same time, I wanted this. I wanted Mason so bad that I felt like I would die if he didn't fuck me. I tilted my head back and parted my lips as he worked me over.

"That's it, baby." Mason grunted as he filled me again. "The way your little pussy feels wrapped around me is like nothing else I've had before." His fingers reached up to grab my chin. "I haven't been able to come inside another woman since you." Mason slid his lips against mine before he pulled out and flipped me around so that my chest was pressed against the wall. He teased his cock against my slippery entrance. "You want this?" He nipped at my ear while he teased me with the tip.

"God, yes."

Mason plunged inside my aching pussy again and when he did I came. I clenched tightly around his shaft as I clawed at the wall and cried out Mason's name. He just kept going, pushing me right into another orgasm. I arched back onto his dick and tried to spread my legs farther, wanting more, needing more.

Mason growled into my neck. "That's it, London." His hand slipped up in front of my dress as he searched for my nipple and when he found it, he squeezed and pulled as he moved. "So damn good." He wrapped his arm around my waist as he held me in place and when he came, I came again with him. The sounds he made were so raw and sexy that I couldn't stop myself from another climax even if I wanted to.

Sweat dripped from my forehead as Mason pulled his cock from me and spun me around so that his eyes burned into me. I had never seen him look so hungry before and I immediately wanted him again, even though he just made me come three times.

Mason moved closer to my face and I thought he might kiss me, but he didn't. "Did I hurt you?" he asked softly. "You know I can be rough sometimes." His eyes searched my face.

"I like it when you're rough," I reminded him and watched as his lips twitched as he tried not to smile.

Mason's arm wrapped around my waist again as he nibbled on my bottom lip. "How about another round?" He murmured before he pulled my dress up and over my head. Mason ran his tongue down my neck and down to my taut nipples where he sucked hard on the left one before moving to the right.

I funneled my hands into Mason's dark hair. I whimpered as he licked and lapped at my tits. God, I loved when he did that. He pushed my thighs apart with his knee before he dropped to the floor and looked up at me. I watched as he ran his tongue up and over my clit while his eyes stayed on mine. I knew how Mason liked it. Dirty, rough and while he was in control. My hands came up to my nipples as he gripped my thighs.

"You taste so sweet," he murmured into my pussy and continued his slow, painful assault on me, not seeming to care that his own cum was mixed in with my juices. Mason's tongue swirled around my wet folds as he pulled one leg up over his shoulder before he pulled back. "You want me to fuck you again?" His face was covered in wetness and my belly fluttered with desire and a little something more.

I whimpered at his question and without another word, he scooped me up against his thick chest to carry me toward the bedroom.

<u>Chapter Nine</u>

Mason

I placed London on my bed before I instructed her to lie down. Christ, she was beautiful even if she didn't think so. I watched as her chest moved up and down as her breathing got faster. "You tell me at any time if you need to stop or if it's too much," I told her. "Okay?"

London nodded. "Okay." Her eyes were wide when I started to climb onto the bed.

I smiled as I pressed my body over hers. "So fucking beautiful," I murmured as I took one nipple into my mouth. London whimpered as I brought my hand up to play and pull with the left one as I sucked hard and long with the right. Her hands came up to pull at my hair and the longer I stayed on her tits, the rougher London got with me. I looked up to find her watching me as I ran my tongue around her peaked nipple. I knew how she felt about herself, that her boobs were too small, which they weren't, her body wasn't good enough, which it is, and I wanted to prove her wrong.

I licked my way across her chest to the left tit. "Still good?" I nipped softly with my teeth at her erect nipple.

"Mason."

My cock jumped when London moaned my name like that. "I know, baby, all in good time," I assured her as I rolled the right nipple between my fingers. "Let's get you onto all fours now." I pulled myself away from her body. I put both my hands onto her hips to help turn London on her knees before I lightly slapped her ass with the palm of my hand. She arched her back slightly as a whimper escaped her mouth.

"I need to come, Mason," London begged. "Please, fuck me again."

"Soon," I promised before I stripped off the rest of my clothes. My cock was heavy with its own want as I stared at the woman currently on all fours on my bed. Christ, I was going to fuck her silly right now.

"God, look at how fucking hard you are," London whispered. "Bring yourself over here." Her eyes were wild as she watched me walk back to the bed.

I groaned when London wrapped a slim hand around my cock and brought it to her lips. She slowly ran her tongue around the top before she opened her mouth to swallow me down her throat. I watched as London's mouth moved up and down my shaft until I thought I might burst. I pulled back and wiped the spittle from her lips.

I smirked at her. "My turn." I nudged her legs apart before I lie down on my back underneath her. London's own want was weeping down her legs. "Bring yourself closer to me, you know, like you're going to ride my face," I instructed. I growled as she did exactly as I told her. Then I dragged my tongue right through her wetness and over her clit, tasting her and my own juices. She cried out on contact and bucked against my face. I brought a hand up to palm her ass while I began to lick and lap at her, but what I really wanted was to see how she would react to me touching her ass.

London had said she had done everything, but was that true?

Had she tried anal before? She was currently riding my face and I knew she was going to come soon by the sounds she was making, but I wanted to finish her off good by rimming her little tight hole. I swiped my finger through her wetness before I slowly ran it against her back end.

"Mason." London pushed down against my face. "Holy shit."

Bingo.

I slipped a finger inside her eager pussy before I made it two, and she clenched so tight I wished it was my cock instead. Then I pushed the same finger I used to brush London's ass inside her again and she went off like a firework above me. She came in quivering waves while I lapped at her sweet pussy with my tongue and my own cock twitched and throbbed. When I was sure she was done, I slipped out from underneath her with a dick so fucking hard it hurt.

London was face down on the bed panting, her body covered in a slick sheen of sweat, but I wasn't done with her yet. I pulled her back up and plunged inside her wetness with a driving hunger that I didn't even know that I had. London pushed back against me as she clutched the sheets in front of her. I stretched her, filled her more than I thought possible and God it felt good. I moved faster, harder, and she cried out with every single movement.

She turned to watch me with eyes so hot that I almost came right then. "It's so good," she whispered as I shifted my rhythm. London's eyes fluttered and her mouth fell open, but she kept watching me.

I grabbed her hair without thinking and pulled London up

onto her knees. I let my hand slide up and around her throat, but I didn't tighten it. London whimpered softly as she shoved her backside against me and let my fingers tighten slightly while she slipped a hand down between her legs to rub at her clit. She didn't fight me or try to pull away as we moved together before her moans turned to cries and then screams of pleasure, the tingles ripping through both of us like electricity.

My release caught me by surprise and it was almost violent. London tightened around me at the same time as I poured everything into her. I pulled myself out of her before I collapsed onto the bed, gasping for breath.

"Mason."

London was watching me when I opened my eyes, her head leaning on her hand. "That was fucking amazing." A slight blush filled her cheeks. "I've never—"

"I know, baby." I ran my thumb over her bottom lip. "I've never had a woman here before." The words slipped from my mouth before I could stop them.

London's eyes went wide. "Really?" She started to get up and I knew it was because she was going to cover herself.

I grabbed her arm to pull her against me. "Really." I kissed her lips lightly. "Tell me about these." I touched her stomach and immediately regretted it. The scars were something I was curious about but clearly she didn't want to talk about them. She struggled to get up from the bed.

"Let go of me."

"London, wait. I'm sorry."

"I have to get dressed. Please." London jumped from the bed

and grabbed my shirt from the floor since her dress was still in the other room. I wanted to find and strangle the person who told her she wasn't good enough or pretty enough because even with her hair bleached, London Sullivan was still the most beautiful woman I had ever seen.

I touched her arm. "I'm sorry. It's none of my business. I won't ask again." I tilted London's face up so she had to look at me. It nearly broke my heart when I saw the pain in her eyes. I would double strangle that person.

Tears filled those same big blue eyes. "Why, Mason? Why do you even care?" She tried to get away again, but this time I didn't let go and crushed her against me.

"Because I want to know everything about you." Shit, there it was. Right out in the open.

London looked like she wanted to be anywhere but here right now. That makes two of us, baby. "Wh-what?" she stuttered.

"Don't you get it? I can't get you out of my head, and I don't want you to go anywhere. I can't think of anyone else but you. I eat, sleep and dream of London Sullivan."

"Mason, don't be a dick." London shook her head.

I raised an eyebrow. "Don't believe me? Fine, you can leave." *Please don't go*, I silently begged her.

"I tried to cut my fat off." The voice was so quiet I almost didn't hear her. I almost didn't think I did until I saw the look on London's face.

"I was sixteen years old at the time. I was so depressed, not eating, and I thought it would make me feel better." London pressed her forehead against my chest. "Spoiler alert... it didn't."

She wrapped her arms around me.

"Why on earth did you want to…?" I realized what she had just said. She hadn't been eating. Brooklyn had said her sister had been in and out of the hospital since she was thirteen. "I'm so sorry, baby." I wasn't sure what else I could say to her. I remembered hearing about a girl in school that was bulimic, but that was the only thing I knew about eating disorders.

"I've been doing well for the past few years." London looked up again. "You know, Rand helped pay for my last hospital stint." She giggled. "It was the first time we met, too, and I was in the hospital with a G-tube stuck in my stomach because I wasn't eating and barfing to try to get skinny." Her eyes didn't laugh with her though.

"London." I wasn't sure what to say. What could I say?

"It's fine, Mason. I'm okay. I have medication to help with my depression. I see a shrink twice a week." She untangled herself from me and this time I let her. "You didn't know anything about me. Now you have a little insight into how crazy I am." She started toward the door. "I'm just going to get my underwear," she called over her shoulder.

"Why?" I started after her. "Who said I was done with you yet?" I teased as I tried to take in what London had just told me. It wasn't that I didn't want her around because I did. It was just a lot to handle at once.

London stuck one leg into her underwear and then the other before she shimmied into them. "I can see your brain turning, Mason." She untucked my shirt where it was stuck in the back. "You're regretting letting me stay here." She folded her arms across her chest.

"Truth?" I asked, and she nodded. "It's a lot to compute all at once, baby, but there is no way I would let you leave now." I watched as she realized I was being honest. Something she might not be used to. I had no doubt Brooklyn loved London, but she might not always be honest with her.

"Mason." London's chin trembled when she spoke. "Why are you being so nice to me now?" She shook her head when I tried to move closer. "I don't deserve this."

"I wish you realized you did, baby." I ignored her protests and swooped in to hold her. "So, why don't we make an appointment to take care of this hair?" I teased which caused London to giggle.

"I like that idea," she said.

———

We spent the rest of the afternoon at the mall which wasn't my favorite place in the world, but it wasn't so bad with London around. First stop was the hair salon where she had her hair dyed back to its natural color. Or, what was closest to her natural brown color. Unfortunately due to whatever they used to bleach it so white they had to cut off a lot of it, but I thought it looked cute. Of course, I wasn't much of an expert on hair so it wasn't really up to me to like it.

"It's short." London ran her hands through her waves. She turned her head as she looked at herself in the mirror the hairdresser had given her. "I... I don't think I've had hair this short since I was a kid."

I smiled. "It fits you, baby," I assured her as I rested my hands on her shoulders. "Plus, if you don't like it your hair will grow back," I reminded her.

After that London needed a few clothes, so she dragged me in and out of stores while she tried them on. First stop was Express, where I refused to even step inside. I handed London my credit card and told her to buy whatever she wanted. Twenty minutes later she walked out holding one bag.

One *tiny* little fucking bag.

"That's it?" I pointed to the small bag. "What's in there? Underwear?" I tried to see what was inside, but she pulled it away.

"Buying clothes is not one of my favorite things, Mason." London rolled her eyes. "Oh, Target." She grabbed my arm to guide me toward the superstore. "I love this place."

"I thought you didn't like shopping."

"For clothes, silly." London giggled as she picked up one of those stupid signs that said "Live, Laugh, Love" or whatever on it. "You don't need an excuse to come to Target to shop. You let Target tell *you* what to buy." She broke into a huge smile as she saw a display of back to school notebooks.

Shit, we might be here awhile.

Two hours, and three hundred plus dollars later, we walked out of Target and the mall. I wasn't even exactly sure of everything I had bought, but the smile plastered on London's face was enough to make me not care. She insisted I buy two coffee mugs. One with an "L" for London, and the other with an "M" for Mason. She also picked out a few shorts, some T-shirts, and a few other clothes for herself as well as some odds and ends that she said she needed. She looked happy as fuck, so I didn't care.

On our way back to my place, I asked London if she was hungry. I knew that I was starving and thought maybe we could pick up something on the way home.

"Sure, whatever." She had her feet hanging out the window of my car and wiggled her toes in the wind. "Thanks, by the way."

I patted her thigh. "Of course, baby." I noticed London hadn't flinched when I touched her. Maybe she was relaxing a little around me. Or maybe she was just getting more comfortable with it. Either way, it made my chest tighten in a way I wasn't used to.

"Can we get pizza?"

"I know the best place."

Back at my place with one large pizza, and all the bags inside the apartment, we sat down on the couch to watch television. "So," I asked before I took a bite. "What do you like to watch?" I leaned back against the cushions.

"I don't really watch anything." London placed a napkin on her pizza and I watched as she soaked the grease off. "Don't judge, Mason. I just don't like the extra fat." She took a bite, chewed and then swallowed. "It's just a thing I do." She took another bite.

I wasn't judging, but maybe she was used to people doing

that. "How can you not watch television?" I changed the subject. "No *American Idol? The Bachelor? Big Bang Theory?* Nothing?" I knew the last one was over, but I threw it in there anyway because I liked the reruns when I had the time.

"I watch *Say Yes To The Dress* now and again." A smile pulled at her lips as the blood drained from my face. "I'm kidding, Mason." She chuckled softly and I realized how much I loved the sound of her laugh.

"A movie then?" I suggested instead.

London tucked her feet underneath her legs. "I'm fine with whatever you want to watch, really," she assured me.

We ended up watching *Wedding Crashers* a movie that I had seen a hundred times, but loved and London had never watched at all. She seemed to enjoy it or at least pretended to, but at some point I looked over, and she had fallen asleep on the couch next to me. I turned off the movie, then the television before I put the rest of the pizza away. Next I picked London up into my arms and carried her into the bedroom where I placed her on the bed.

"Movie over?" She looked at me with sleepy eyes. "Did I fall asleep?"

"'Fraid so, baby." I pulled the blanket up around her neck.

London smiled at me before she clutched my shirt between her small fingers. "Stay here until I'm asleep?" She tugged lightly.

Don't do it, Pelletier. You're already in too deep with this girl. She's at your house, in your bed, you went shopping with her... "Of course, London." I heard myself tell her. Watched as she moved over and let me snuggle in next to her. I wrapped my arms around her as she pushed back against my chest and realized that this was probably the first time I had ever just cuddled with a woman.

London's hands found mine and she laced our fingers together. "Today was a good day," she whispered as she began to fall asleep.

I pressed my lips against her hair. "You deserve all good days, baby," I told her.

I stayed there until London fell asleep, just like she asked me to. Then I stayed there until I fell asleep, too.

<u>Chapter Ten</u>

The nightmare jolted me from my sleep in the morning. I woke up screaming, and as I tried to get up out of the bed I stumbled, tangled in the blankets. I felt a hand on my shoulder, and I shrieked in terror before I managed to jump to the floor to press myself against the wall.

"Baby, calm down." Mason's eyes were wide with fright. Shit, had he stayed there the entire night or had I woke him up?

I shook my head. "Don't touch me!" I turned my head as I panted and tried to forget the nightmare. It was always the same. Cooper was always there with his beady eyes and devilish grin pawing at me the way he always did. I wrapped my arms around myself as my body shook with fright.

"It's me." Mason's voice was soft as he held the palms of his hands out in front of him. "You're safe now." He assured me, and before I realized what I was doing, I threw myself at his chest, sobbing.

"I'm sorry," I exclaimed as I cried. "I have these nightmares sometimes, and when I wake up, I often forget where I am. I didn't mean to yell or—"

Mason soothed the back of my head with his hand. "I understand. You don't have to explain anything." I trembled in his arms despite his assurance. "It's not your fault." He gave me a faint smile when I rested my chin on his chest so that I could look up at him. His brown eyes were soft and warm as he touched my face.

"Do you remember the time that you saved me?" I pressed as close to Mason as I could. "From Cooper?" The venom in my voice would always be there when I said his name. "Then carried me back into my room like some knight in shining armor and I asked you to stay with me until I fell asleep? That was probably the day I—" I stopped at the sound of the doorbell and realized I almost told Mason I loved him. "You should probably go see who that is." I took a step back.

"Wait." Mason hooked an arm around my waist. "What were you going to say, baby? The day that you probably what?" We stared at one another before the bell chimed again.

I patted Mason's chest. "Someone really needs you." I winked. "Sounds important, Pelletier," I teased before I finally managed to get away. "I should call Sully anyway. She's been blowing up my phone since I left, and I haven't answered yet. She probably thinks I'm turning tricks on the street again."

Mason's eyebrows dipped.

"I'm kidding."

"Not funny, baby," Mason growled before whoever was at the door began knocking. "Jesus, fuck! I'm coming. Calm your tits." He turned to head to the door to find out who was outside.

I threw on a new shirt that Mason had bought me as well as a new pair of shorts before I ran a hand through my hair. It would take some getting used to it being so short, but it was kind of cute. I really needed a shower, but maybe after breakfast, if there *was* breakfast, I could do that.

"Hey." Mason knocked lightly on the door. "You, uh, might want to come out there before your sister calls the cops on me," he joked, but his eyes were pinched.

"What?" I stomped into the living room to find Brooklyn in the doorway. "Seriously?"

"You haven't returned my calls or texts, London! What was I supposed to do?" Her eyes moved over my body. "Your hair looks really great." Brooklyn tilted her head. "Lon, can we talk?"

"We are talking." I tilted my head to look over at Mason.

He nodded. "Right, let me just go take a walk so you two can have some alone time." Mason grabbed his phone as big sis finally stepped into the apartment.

I flashed him a smile as he shut the door. "So, talk?" I folded my arms over my chest.

"He's taking care of you?" Sully asked as she looked over the apartment.

I raised my eyebrows. "I'm not a baby, Brooklyn. I can dress and feed myself. He took me shopping, we got my hair done. Are you worried that Mason isn't going to know how to handle me if something happened?" I sat down on the couch and crossed my legs.

"Yes," Sully admitted before she sat down next to me. "I love you, you know that, right?" She sighed. "Mason isn't your boyfriend, and I know you've always had a crush on him, but he isn't going to change for you. We already talked about that. He's not a good guy, Lon. He doesn't love you, and you can enjoy playing house for now, but—"

I shot up off the couch as my anger began to boil over. "Stop it! This isn't about Mason, is it? This is about the fact that I'm no longer under your house or your rules. You can't stand the fact that I'm on my own, doing my own thing, and you can't tell me what to do!" I shouted at her. "Mason is kind to me. He cares about me." I pulled up the front of my shirt to point at my scars. "I told him all about what I did, and he didn't run. He didn't freak out or try to kick me out." I laughed bitterly. "You don't care about me."

"London, I do. I've always cared about you. I've done everything I possibly could for you. I love you more than you'll ever know." Brooklyn stood up. "I want you to be happy, find someone who will love you, have a family, but Mason isn't that person."

"I love him."

Brooklyn's eyes went wide before she shook her head back and forth so hard her ponytail slapped her in the face. "No, no, you don't. Think about what you just said..." She bit down on her bottom lip. "Look, you like playing house with him?" Brooklyn was trying to gather herself together. I knew how my sister worked. "It's fun, I totally understand that, but think about *who* you're talking about."

"I don't understand why you hate Mason so much," I challenged her. "What did he do that was so horrible, so terrible that you don't want me to be with him?" There was something Sully wasn't telling me. Was it because Mason had been friends with Cooper? Or was it the whole Apple thing?

"You need to respond to my text messages next time." Brooklyn ignored my questions. "Just let me know you're alive, okay?" She smoothed down the front of her shirt. "I miss you. You can come home when you're ready." She didn't try to hug me because she knew I wouldn't want that.

I nodded. "Fine. Thanks." I pressed my lips together as I followed Brooklyn outside. Mason was standing by her car and I realized it was because Rand was in there and RJ was in the back. "Tell RJ I miss him." I missed playing with him. I raised a hand to Rand, who was waving at me.

Mason made his way back to where I was as he slowly ran his hand through his hair. I admired how good he looked just dressed in his pajama pants and I realized I had told my sister that I loved Mason. I didn't even hesitate. It wasn't a lie, but I knew she was right. He would never feel the same way, would never commit to me, and even if he did? I couldn't have children. Not after all the horrible things I had done to my body with my starving and purging myself. Mason would want someone who could give him healthy boys to follow in his footsteps.

"You two alright?" He shut the door as we went back inside.

"Sure, best friends forever."

"Baby."

"What, Mason? What do you want me to say?" I suddenly realized I should have left with them. I shouldn't be here because I was going to end up with a broken heart and all alone.

Mason put his hands on my shoulders. Not too hard, not too rough, but just enough so that I knew he was there. "What did she say? Talk to me, London, I want to know what you're thinking." His brown eyes searched my blues.

"That I should come home. What else would she say?" I ducked under his shoulder, but he grabbed me and pushed me back against the wall. "Let go," I demanded.

"You seem to want to fight with me right now." Mason's eyes narrowed as he pushed his nose against me. "Is that what you do, baby?" I could feel his thick, hard chest against my nonexistent breasts.

"I'll scream."

A smile slipped up his model lips. "Go ahead, but I don't think my half-deaf elderly neighbors will hear you." Mason's lips slid against mine as he spoke.

"Fine, you want to know what Sully said." I stuck out my chin. "You're bad for me. You'll never be my boyfriend or settle down with me. You'll only hurt me, so she just wants to protect me."

Mason raised his hand and slowly traced his finger down my face, over my lips and continued down the middle of my chest. Then he gripped my hip so tight it hurt, but all it did was send a sick thrill throughout my body. "Is that what you think? Because if I didn't want you or care about you." His tongue rolled over the seam of my lips. "I wouldn't have brought you here."

Then his mouth was on mine before I could say a word. Kisses so cruel that they devoured my will to resist, and I could feel his hardness against my stomach. I got up onto my toes, trying to get more, *needing* to get more of Mason, as his hands tugged and pulled at my hair. Our tongues circled together as my hands gripped his broad shoulders and all I could think about was getting him inside me.

"So, baby." Mason's eyes were full of need. "I need to take a shower. You feel like taking one with me? I know how dirty I am right now."

I nodded. "I think I'm dirty, too," I said before I followed him into the bathroom.

———

After our fun and sex-filled shower, Mason told me he had to head down to the race shop to go over a few things with his car owner. He invited me to come with him, but I politely declined. He said he wouldn't be long, maybe two or three hours, and to make myself at home.

I had a lot of unanswered text messages to return. I started off with Rush, then Nola, and finally Tessa. I was actually surprised to hear from Tessa because after what happened the night of the party? I figured she was probably scared as hell and didn't want to be my friend.

London: *Thanks for checking in on me. I'm good. I was afraid you didn't want to hang out again.*

I went into the kitchen to get something to drink when she texted me back.

Tessa: *Are you kidding? That was the most fun I've had in forever. Is Mason your boyfriend? I can't believe your brother-in-law is Rand Shepard. I'm so jealous.*

Oh, shit. I guess everyone around here was a damn NASCAR fan.

London: *Uh, no. Mason and I are just...*

What did I tell her? I didn't want to leave Tessa hanging, but

I couldn't lie.

London: *We're just kind of friends, but bumping uglies. IDK what you want to call it.*

I popped open the soda and moved around the apartment before I realized there was a back porch. How damn fancy was this? I slipped outside to sit down.

Tessa: *Want to hang out? I'm off today.*

Yes, yes, I did. I had nothing to do but sit around and wait for Mason while he did God only knew what so I told her to come get me, the address and then texted Mason.

London: *I'm going out with a friend.*

Mason: *Friend?*

London: *A girlfriend. Tessa.*

Mason: *Where? How long?*

What was he, my dad now? Jesus. We weren't roommates, hell we weren't even a couple. I wasn't even sure what we were going to do, but I could make up a little white lie.

London: *A movie*

Mason: *What movie? Where?*

I groaned as I stomped my foot and saw Tessa pull into the parking lot. I waved as she drove over to me. "Where is the closest movie theater so I can tell Mason? He's got major dad vibes right now." I rolled my eyes.

"That is kinky as fuck." Tessa chuckled. "Tell him we're going to Mansfield. It's about twenty minutes from here."

I texted the information to Mason and when he didn't respond I figured that he believed me until my phone buzzed.

Mason: *You better not be lying to me, baby. If you are, I'll spank your ass until it's red and raw.*

I pushed my legs together as an ache built between my thighs.

London: *Okay, daddy.*

I giggled to myself as Tessa drove along.

"What's so funny?" Tessa asked as she glanced over at me.

I smiled. "I'm going to be in some serious trouble when I get home." I rolled the window down to feel the breeze in my hair. "And, you know what? I don't even care."

Chapter Eleven

London was lying to me. She was lying to me, and now I couldn't concentrate on anything my car owner, Peter Baker or crew chief, Ned Simmons, was talking about right now. I knew that it had something to do with my grandfather, Henry, because he was also part car owner, but hardly ever came around unless he had to be and for that I was forever grateful. I bounced my knee up and down as I fidgeted in the chair, and waited for this meeting to be over.

"Mason, son, are you listening to me?" Peter was watching me with narrowed eyes.

Shit, no. "Uh, sorry, sir. I have a lot on my mind right now." I glanced up at the clock on the wall again.

Ned sighed. "What's her name, Mason?" He smiled at me.

"Excuse me?"

"The look on your face says girl. You keep looking at the clock, you were texting someone before, and you haven't stopped moving since you sat down. It's obviously a woman." Ned raised his eyebrows as he sat back in his chair.

I looked between the two of them. I had been working with both men since I started racing in the NASCAR cup series. Ned had been almost like a father to me without having to be, and Peter had stepped in to help me get out of more jams than I cared to remember. The least I could do was be honest with them right now.

"London. Her name is London Sullivan."

Ned sat back in his chair and folded his arms across his chest. "I've known you a very long time, son, but I've never seen you act like this. Not about anyone." He sat forward again. "She must be something special if she's got you all tied up in knots like that."

"I can't stop thinking about her every single minute of every single day." The words tumbled from my mouth before I could stop them. "I want to spend all my free time with London. I want to be the air that she breathes, the sun that shines on her skin and the reason she smiles all day long." Holy shit, who was I right now?

Peter nodded. "That's called love, son. You're in love with the girl." He gave me a knowing smile.

I shook my head. "No fucking way." But the longer I thought about it, the more it made sense.

And the more it scared the living *shit* out of me.

"London wouldn't happen to be the sister of Brooklyn Sullivan, would she? The one Rand married?" Ned asked as he stood up to empty out his coffee cup.

Smart fuckers these two, but then again gossip in the garage was worse than any high school shit I had ever dealt with. I wasn't surprised that they figured it out.

I nodded. "Yes, that would be her." I watched as the two men exchanged looks.

Ned chuckled. "Go then. Be back tomorrow morning so we can go over the Darlington race," he called out to me as I sprinted from the room.

I wasn't sure where I was going or what I was doing. Love?

That was something I never thought would happen to me. I slammed my hand against the steering wheel. "Shit!" I yelled out into the empty car. I found myself driving around for what felt like hours when it was only about twenty minutes and finally pulled into Apple's driveway.

"Isn't this a surprise?" She opened the door for me and then walked back from where she had been. "How's domestic bliss going?" she called out.

I closed the door and followed her. "I need your help with something." I sat down on a chair that was so worn the stuffing was starting to come out. Again, if Apple would only take the money I offered her, she wouldn't have to deal with this.

Apple's eyebrows dipped. "With?" She was wearing a dress that was at least one size too small, her oversized breasts pushed up to emphasize her cleavage. Her blonde ponytail shifted as she tilted her head. "You fucking love her." She closed her eyes. "Holy shit, Mason, what are you doing?"

I hung my head. "I don't know, Megan." I sat back and stared up at the ceiling.

"Don't call me that," Apple hissed before she stood up and moved over to where I was sitting. "Have you told her? Don't be a dick about it, Mason." She ruffled my hair playfully as she went into the kitchen, and I could hear the flick of the lighter as she lit her cigarette.

I got up to follow her. "Those things are going to kill you. Think about your daughter." I watched as she blew smoke out the window.

Apple rolled her eyes, but then quickly stubbed the cigarette out in the ashtray. "What are you going to do about London, huh? Are you going to pussy out or are you going to man up?" She folded her arms over her chest.

"I was hoping you could help me."

"You think that *I* have the answers? I did that once, Mason, and it didn't work out for me." She rolled her eyes. "You're different. You're a good guy whether you want to believe it or not." She leaned her hip against the counter as she looked up at me. "Tell her."

"What if London doesn't feel the same? What if she rejects me?" The thought terrified me.

Apple's lips turned up into a smirk. "Something tells me that girl isn't going to do that," she told me. "Besides, if she does, she'll be making the biggest mistake of her life," she teased.

Apple and I talked a little more about how I should tell London how I felt, and then I went home. I texted London to tell her to have her friend bring her home, and on my way back I stopped at a little lingerie place I had actually never stepped foot in before. Trust me when I say I wanted to buy everything for London, but instead I just picked out a sexy sheer baby doll that matched the color of her eyes. Then I sat down on the couch and waited.

London stopped dead in her tracks when she saw me waiting. She stared at me with big, wide eyes as she took me in. "You smell like cigarette smoke." She pouted. "Where did you go? Who were you with?" she demanded.

"Really? You want to fight with me right now?" This wasn't going the way I had hoped.

"Yes."

"Where were *you*?" I shot back. "You didn't go to the movies, baby. We both know that." I stood up.

"Just out."

"That so?" I was close enough to touch her, but I didn't. She smelled like something sweet. Something I wanted to eat.

London jutted her chin at me. "Yes, Tessa, and I just went out for a drive. We didn't do anything." She actually looked scared.

I chuckled. "Strip off all your clothes, baby," I demanded. When London didn't move, I moved so that we were chest to chest. "Take them off or I'll take them off for you."

"Not until you tell me who you were with." London's eyes blazed with something between hate and heat. She knew exactly where I had been. She also knew that Apple and I were nothing more than friends.

"You want me to say her name? You want to start a fight with me, baby?" I gripped her jaw between my fingers. "I was with Apple." Fire blazed in those blue eyes.

"I hate you." London struggled to get away from me. "I won't do this with you. I won't be your fuck toy while you go see someone else." She pushed at me with the palms of her hands.

"I'm not fucking her, London. I'm sticking my dick in one woman and that's you," I reminded her. I watched as she ran past me into the bedroom and I slowly followed her as she started to throw her things into a bag. "What are you doing?" I leaned against the frame.

"Leaving."

"Is that so?" I asked as she stopped to look at me.

London nodded. "Yes, I'm not... what are you doing?" she asked as I walked into the room, scooped her up into my arms and then sat down on the bed. I placed her face down over my lap.

"I believe you said I could spank you." I grew hard as a rock at the thought and I pulled up the bottom of the dress she had on.

"Wh-what?" London stammered. "Mason, you can't..." she cried out once I slapped her ass over her underwear. She turned to stare at me. "Again." She panted.

I smirked as I pulled her little white panties down. Her small, perfect ass was already pink from where I had slapped her. She squirmed against me before she raised herself up slightly. "Eager, aren't we?" I teased before I brought my hand back down again.

"Mason." She moaned my name the moment I made contact with her backside.

"Fucking Christ, London." I brought her up onto my lap. "I didn't hurt you, did I?" I kissed her lips lightly.

She shook her head. "No." She reached for the button on my jeans. "Fuck me, Mason." London pulled down the zipper and reached inside my pants to grip my dick in her hands. "I need you inside me. Now." She pushed me back onto the bed and I watched as she pulled her dress up over her head.

Her pink nipples poked through the fabric of her bra as she tried not to cross her arms over her chest. "Fuck, you are gorgeous." I let my eyes rake down London's body. "Sit on my dick, baby." I sat up on my arms. "Show me how much you want me inside you." Then I reached down to tear her underwear right from her.

London straddled my waist and began to ease herself over the head of my cock. I groaned as I felt just how wet, and eager she was to take me inside her. Her little nipples dragged over my chest and I couldn't help but take one inside my mouth to suck it right through the fabric. London arched back to give me more, her tight pussy rippling and pulsing around me as our hips came to rest together.

"Baby, you feel so good." I met her eyes just as she began to rotate her hips in slow circles. She began to move faster, faster, and faster until she cried out as her first orgasm shook through her tiny body frame. I hooked an arm around her waist so that I could flip London onto her back and fuck her.

London met my thrusts with her own while her little whimpers grew louder as I slicked my cock in and out of her wetness. Pleasure drenched over both of us while she clawed desperately at my back. I leaned down to bury my face against her neck as the sensation sizzled through me.

"Come again for me, baby," I whispered into her skin as I thrust in and out. "Fuck." I grunted softly.

London exploded like the morning sun underneath me. Her body writhed and shook as she screamed my name so loud that I was pretty sure my elderly neighbors might actually hear her this time. I couldn't hold back and I came, too, my seed coating her sweet little pussy like I hadn't come in months.

After we were done, I stayed there for a second, and then

met London's eyes. "I'm going to tell you something and I don't want you to freak out." I brushed some strands of hair from her forehead.

"What?" Panic covered her face.

I smiled. "I love you," I whispered. "I know it's too soon or crazy, but I realized it today, I love you, London Sullivan. I don't want to be without you."

"What?"

She was freaking out. I saw it all over her face, her eyes, even her body. "London, it's okay if you don't feel the same way." It wasn't but I could deal with that later.

London shook her head. "No, no, no." She pushed at me so that I had no choice but to move away. I watched as she picked up the dress she was just wearing and pulled it back on over her head. "You don't love me. You're just..."

"I'm what, baby?" I zipped up my pants as I climbed up off the bed. "Not good enough?"

"What?" London exclaimed. "No! You're *too* good for me. Mason, I'm fucking not good enough for you! I'm never going to be able to be that wife. Or have babies or give you the life you want. You need someone who is normal. Someone that can give you everything that you want. You *can't* love me." She wrapped her arms around herself.

"Who said that? You're perfect." I took a step forward, but she only took one back. "Alright, we can talk about this." I felt my heart twist inside my chest and I honestly was starting to feel like I might be having a panic attack. Was she fucking rejecting me? I didn't think this through before I spilled my guts.

London shook her head. "I think that I should go back to Sully's so that you can go back to your normal life."

"You're my normal, London Sullivan," I whispered.

"Please, Mason. Just let me go." London's voice was sad. "I'm going to text Sully to come get me."

I could fight London. I should fight her. I could tell her I didn't give two shits what she thought and I wouldn't let her go. Except I didn't. I fucking stood there like a complete and total asshole and watched the first woman I ever loved walk out of my life.

––––––––––

Three weeks later, I was a complete and total mess. I hadn't finished a race or felt like I slept more than a couple hours a night. I was losing my damn mind over London, and she didn't seem to even care.

"You're a fucking idiot."

Rand wasn't telling me something I didn't already know as we sat around the fire pit in Lake and Harper's backyard. I gave him the bird as I swallowed from my bottle of beer.

Lake snickered as he flipped a couple of burgers. "You're a little touchy for someone who told me he wasn't in love." He pointed the spatula at me. "But, now you admit it." He flashed me a wicked smile.

I rolled my eyes. "Get bent, asshole." I drained the last of my beer. "She doesn't want me anyway so it doesn't even matter."

"I wouldn't be so sure of that." Rand swung his arm around Brooklyn's shoulder as she walked over to him. She looked at me with ice in her dark eyes. "She hasn't left her room since she got home. Brooklyn brings her food and water, but she won't come out. She just sits there writing music and crying."

"What the fuck do you mean, crying?" It wasn't like I hadn't thought about driving to Rand's every damn minute of every day and taking her home with me. I was just trying to respect London's wishes.

Harper came over and placed a bowl on the table. She glanced over at Brooklyn before she touched my arm. "You need to give her time."

"I'm trying."

"My sister thinks you deserve better," Brooklyn piped up. "I disagree, but tomato, tomahto. The two of you need to figure things out on your own. Try talking maybe?"

"She won't answer any of my calls or text messages which kind of reminds me of when the two of you broke up once. I'm not going to wait *three years* to get back together with her." The thought of not seeing London or talking to her for that long made me sick to my stomach.

Brooklyn sighed before she stood up. "She told me." Her eyes were still cool when they met mine.

"What do you mean, she told you?" I shook my head. "I didn't do anything to London. I told you that." Now I was starting to get really pissed.

"About Apple." Brooklyn raised her hand before I could say

anything else. "I'm not mad anymore, but really? Mason, she tried to break up Rand and me. Now you're bringing her into London's life, too?"

"We're fucking friends."

"Really?"

I stood up. "You know what? I made a promise to Cooper to take care of her before he fucking died. He was a fucking idiot. I'm sorry you hate me because of that, because of Apple. I'm sorry that the bastard knocked Apple up when he was supposed to marry you. I'm sorry he fucked you both over because neither one of you deserved that." The words were out of my mouth before I could stop them. The silence that followed was nearly deafening, but it was too late to stop now. "Apple has been there for me when I needed a friend and vice versa. I needed her help, and I took her advice which clearly blew up in my damn face. I couldn't go to you." I pointed at Rand. "Or you." I pointed at Finn who had just walked in with Mia.

"Me?" He blinked.

"Fuck this shit." I dumped my beer out before I dumped it into the recycle container. "I'm out of here." I started to head toward the house so I could leave. I had had enough of my judgmental so-called fucking friends.

"Mason, wait."

I turned around to find Brooklyn running after me. "I'm sorry," she whispered.

"I'm sorry I said that. I shouldn't have sprung the baby thing—"

She shook her head. "I know about the baby." She almost

looked embarrassed.

"What?"

"Funny story." Brooklyn laughed but it wasn't real. "I came down to North Carolina once to surprise my so-called fiancé at the time, and I caught him with a girl. I didn't put two and two together that it was Apple until just now, but she was pregnant. Maybe only a few months, but they were fucking talking about baby shit when I showed up at his place."

My eyes went wide. "Shit, I'm sorry." I wasn't sure what else I should say.

Brooklyn waved a hand at me. "Not your fault." She shook her head. "Neither one of them saw me and I never told Cooper about it. I had planned to break up with him the next weekend, but..." Her voice trailed off.

I didn't have to finish that for her. We all knew what happened. "I should have told you Cooper was a piece of shit, but I was afraid he would drop me from the cool kids club." I saw Rand watching us. "I think we should go back to your husband."

Brooklyn turned her head to wave at her husband. "Come back to the party." She put her hand on my arm. "We can talk about London and maybe work on how you can get her back." She smiled at me.

I followed Brooklyn back to the party and sat down in the chair that I had vacated just a minute or so ago. Turns out she didn't hate me like I thought she did and maybe things were looking up. Or at least I hoped they were.

Chapter Twelve

London

It's been three weeks. Three weeks and I can still hear Mason's voice in my head telling me that he loves me. Yet, I refused to answer his text messages or his phone calls. I expected him to show up at the house, but after a week went by I realized that wasn't going to happen.

He was probably balls deep inside Apple right now.

The thought made me want to throw up as I sat by the window in my bedroom with the lit cigarette in my hand. I hadn't actually smoked it, but just having it there made me feel better. I felt like such a shell of myself that at least this made me feel a little more normal.

I was home alone since Rand and Sully had gone to some barbecue at Harper's place. They had invited me, well Sully begged, but I said no. I knew that Mason would be there and I didn't want to see him. Okay, that was a lie because I did, but I wanted him to come to me. Climb up the terrace and save me from... from what? Myself? No one could save me from me.

Not only was I ignoring Mason's texts, but I was ignoring everyone else's, too. Tessa, Rush, and Nola had all texted me at least twice a day for the past three weeks, but all I did was read them. I didn't have it in me to respond. I just sat upstairs in my room, writing sad love songs, and sleeping most of the day.

And, crying. I don't remember crying so much in my entire life. I'm surprised that I wasn't dehydrated from all the tears I had lost.

The sound of my phone dancing across my desk caught my attention, so I stubbed out my cigarette and went over to check my phone.

Tessa: *I'm on my way to your sister's place. I went by your boyfriend's, but he told me you moved out. Are you okay?*

Shit! I ran into the bathroom to see just how terrible I looked. The bags under my eyes were big enough to carry groceries in, my hair looked like it hadn't been brushed in days, and I couldn't remember the last time I changed my pajamas. Which also meant I probably hadn't showered in a while either.

Ew.

London: *You don't need to come over. We broke up. I'm going to be okay.*

I quickly typed back so that Tessa wouldn't make an extra trip here. I didn't want her to see me like this. I looked like some extra on The *Walking Dead* right now.

Tessa: *Too late because I'm already here.*

Sure enough, when I moved back into my room, I saw headlights from her car as she drove up the driveway. "Fuck," I muttered under my breath. It was too late to change, so I finger-combed my hair and hurried down to the front door.

Tessa stopped to stare at me as her eyes took me in. "You look like crap. Sorry, I know we're not best friends yet, but seriously. What did he do?" She moved in to hug me, but I took a step back.

"I... uh... haven't showered in a couple days." I held up my hands. "It's probably not the best idea."

"Girl, it's fine." Tessa charged forward and wrapped her

arms around me. I immediately went stiff, even though I tried not to. I patted her back lightly, but I knew this was coming off extremely awkward. She pulled back to look me in the eyes. "You don't like to be touched, huh?" She smiled. "I'm sorry; you should have just told me. I wouldn't have tried to smother you. I'm a big hugger, but I think you kind of figured that out."

"It's not something I want to bring up the first time I meet someone." I stuck out my hand. "Hi, I'm London. I'm from Connecticut, I love country music, and I don't like to be touched." I giggled softly. "Thanks for understanding." I motioned for her to follow me into the living room.

"That's what friends are for, London." Tessa sat down in one of the oversized chairs. "You don't have to tell me what happened. Mason just said that you moved out." She started to chew on her bottom lip. "He's super cute. Did he fuck you over? Should I go put sugar in his gas tank? Take the air out of his tires?" Her eyes glittered with evilness. "Maybe set the mistress's house on fire?" Tessa's whole face lit up. "I'm good with shit like that, you know, if you need someone to do it."

I laughed loud and hard before I answered. "Remind me never to piss you off. No, it's fine," I assured her. "Mason didn't cheat on me. Well, at least, that's what he told me. Things between us are super complicated. Hey." I stood up. "You want to get drunk with me?" I went into the kitchen to get two glasses and a bottle of wine. Then I went back into the living room.

"Define complicated." Tessa asked as she watched me pour two glasses of wine. She thanked me when I handed her one.

"Well, I mean, he's Rand's best friend, but my sister hates

him. I've had a crush on him for a long time, and we slept together at a friend's wedding." I left out the part about how I went after him, how he saved me from Cooper because that was our little secret.

"One-night stands are always complicated no matter how hard you try." Tessa sipped her wine. "You really like him." She placed her glass on the table.

I blushed. "Is it that obvious?" I sighed softly. "Mason is... he's too good for me."

"Bullshit."

"Tessa, you've only known me a short time," I reminded her.

"You are good enough for Mason, London. Why can't you see that?" She tilted her head. "Someone told you that you weren't good enough? Not for Mason, but just not good enough in general."

I felt like Tessa was suddenly crawling around inside my head, and I didn't like how it felt. "Could we talk about something else?" I needed to change the subject.

"How about we talk about the hot guy I met this morning at my other job? Holy shit! He was a total babe." Tessa giggled as she finished her glass of wine. "Like I want to accidentally walk in on him when he's naked and pretend I didn't know he was in the room kind of hot." Her ears turned red as she spoke.

Tessa worked as a hotel maid as well as at the liquor store. She claimed she didn't mind, but I had a feeling she might be hiding something, too.

I raised my eyebrows. "And?" I waited for her to go on.

She fell back against the chair. "It's been awhile since I've been with a man." She giggled loudly. "He had the bluest eyes, all these tattoos, and mmm..." She shook her head.

"Did you get his name? Or a number?"

Tess shook her head. "I haven't even spoken to him yet. He walks around with this 'talk to me and I'll kill you' look on his face." She sighed softly. "I've been trying to make up some sort of excuse, but so far no luck."

"You should go for it." I finished off my glass of wine. "I mean, why not? You probably won't see him again."

Eventually Tessa and I ended up going upstairs to my room so that I wouldn't have to deal with Sully when she got home. I asked Tessa if she wanted to stay over since I didn't think it would be a good idea for her to drive with the wine we had been drinking and she agreed. I'm not sure what time Sully and Rand got home because we were asleep, but I know that she checked on me.

She always checked on me.

Tessa woke me up in the morning. "Does your sister cook breakfast for you every morning?" she asked as I sat up.

"No," I assured her. "She's only doing it because you're here. Don't get me wrong, Sully is a great sister. I don't give her enough credit for everything she has done for me." I swung my legs over the bed. "I should take a shower. I feel so nasty." Honestly, I don't remember the last time I washed myself.

"I'll wait." Tessa sat back down on the guest bed. I was

warming up to this room.

I shook my head. "No, you should go downstairs. Get some coffee." I needed five minutes to myself.

Tessa looked like she wanted to fight me, but she didn't. "Don't leave me alone too long. I'm not good with kids." She stood back up.

"Are you kidding? RJ is the best kid on the planet."

Once Tessa had disappeared, I hurried into the bathroom. I stripped off all my clothes and turned on the water as hot as it would go before I stepped in. I still wasn't used to my short hair. I liked it, but I wasn't sure I would keep it like this. I washed and scrubbed myself until I was pretty sure I hadn't missed anything. Then I dried off, lotioned up my skin, and went to put on some clean clothes.

I found a cute little pair of denim shorts that I paired with a blue tank top. I put them on before I finally skipped downstairs.

There was a giant stack of chocolate chip pancakes in the middle of the counter, with what looked like blueberry ones next to that. There was a pile of bacon sky high on the plate next to that, as well as sausage, eggs, and waffles further down. Jesus, someone was hungry this morning.

"Hope you're hungry," Rand called to me from the kitchen table. "Your sister has been cooking up a storm this morning. She was up before the crack of dawn." He poured a ridiculous amount of syrup on his pancakes. "Now she's downstairs folding laundry." He started to cut through his food.

"Your sister is the best." Tessa had a cup of coffee in her hand. "If I eat even half of this food, I'm going to gain ten pounds, but it's so worth it," she teased.

I saw the look on Rand's face at Tessa's comment, but I let it go. I was used to people saying shit that they didn't realize would mean more to me than they knew. Tessa had no clue about my eating disorder and I kind of wanted to keep it that way.. "Right?" I coughed out a laugh as I grabbed two plates and handed one to her. "I don't remember the last time I was able to eat breakfast like this." She piled her plate high with food before she sat down. "The hotel has a continental breakfast that serves muffins and day-old Danish." She wrinkled her nose.

I took a pancake as well as a couple strips of bacon, filled a cup full of coffee and sat down. "Rand." I waited until I had my brother-in-law's attention. "Are you sure Sully isn't pregnant?"

Rand nearly snorted coffee out of his nose. He managed to compose himself and blotted his mouth with a napkin. "Say what now?" His blue eyes were wide.

"Pregnant. You know a baby?" I cut my blueberry pancake into tiny pieces before I dropped a little maple syrup over it.

"Why?" He looked like he had lost his appetite. In fact, Rand looked like he might throw up everything he just ate.

I batted my eyes at him innocently. "Well, the cooking for one thing. When she was pregnant with RJ—" Just at that exact moment my nephew came flying into the kitchen wearing his favorite pair of sneakers, you know the ones with flashing lights, at top speed. Or at least, the top speed of an almost four-year-old.

"Daddy!" He climbed right up into Rand's lap. "Mama said we were getting a pool. Are we getting a pool? Can I swim in it? I don't know how to swim. Can you teach me?" He blew out at least ten or twenty more questions that I sort of ignored.

Tessa kneed me lightly under the table. "Are you serious about your sister?" she asked softly. "Or are you just messing with him?" She crunched on a piece of bacon.

The basement door flew open and my sister appeared. "Good morning, girls." Sully smiled happily at us. "I hope you both slept well." She had the laundry basket on one hip, but as she turned the three of us, Rand, Tessa, and I all tried to catch a glimpse of her stomach. If she was pregnant, she wouldn't be showing yet. She and Rand hadn't been back together that long.

"Darlin', this food is perfect," Rand praised his wife.

Gag. I wouldn't want my husband to treat me like that in front of everyone. Not that I wanted to get married because again, the whole infertile, scarred for life thing.

Thanks, Coop.

Brooklyn dropped a kiss on the top of his head. "Thanks, baby." She looked at him with so much love in her eyes that I felt like I might throw up. Then she began to put a plate together for RJ and then helped him up into his booster seat so he could eat his breakfast. Then she sat down next to Rand.

"RJ said something about a pool?" I had to change the subject.

"We're thinking about it," Rand said. "I mean, we have plenty of room in the back yard, and I've been wanting to tear that damn shed down, too, which would give us much more room."

Ah, the infamous shed. It wasn't really a shed though. It was more like a tiny house in the backyard that you didn't talk about or even mention. Why? Well, Rand had it built for his brother, Eli, who had, at one point, been his best friend, and his mentor. Eli had struggled with addiction and disappeared years ago. Rand took it really hard, but Brooklyn had helped him come back from that. As well as a lot of other things.

Tessa stood up and placed her plate in the sink. "I hate to eat and run, but I have to go. I'll be late to work if I don't leave now. Thanks for having me." She nodded at Sully and Rand.

"Of course, Tessa." Sully nodded.

"Text me," I told her. "We'll hang out this weekend if you aren't working."

Once Tessa was gone Rand turned to look at Brooklyn. "Before we talk any more about this pool, darlin', I need to know one thing." He leaned closer to her. "Are you pregnant?"

Sully's eyes went wide. "Where did you get that idea?" Then she focused on me. "Really, Lon?" She shook her head. "I'm just happy. Just because I'm cooking and cleaning doesn't mean I'm pregnant."

"Sure, I understand." I rinsed off my plate and put it with Tessa's. "I'm going back upstairs."

"Are you doing better?" Brooklyn asked. "You seem better. I don't want to push or anything."

I nodded. "I'll be alright," I told her.

I realized I hadn't thought about Mason for a little while and it felt good. Maybe I wasn't going to die without him. Maybe I *would* be okay if he moved on. If I moved on. I just needed time to tell.

Chapter Thirteen

London

The rest of the summer flew by faster than I thought possible. Of course, it didn't help that Sully and Tessa kept me busy. I had started to think that they got together and planned it that way. As a way for me not to think about Mason or to not run into him. Because I knew that there were times he was at the house or that Rand was probably watching a NASCAR race, but all of a sudden Sully wanted to go shopping or Tessa suggested we go to the movies.

It felt nice to have people that cared about me like that.

Not that I didn't think about Mason all the time. I didn't go all those years obsessing, planning and scheming to get him to fuck me to just forget about him that quickly. Yet, if he loved me the way he claimed to, he could have tried harder to get me back.

In the beginning Mason had texted me nonstop, and I almost changed my phone number. He wanted to talk to me, he was sorry he scared me, but I never responded to a single one. I was serious about the fact that he deserved someone else. Someone better with fewer issues.

I wasn't sure Mason had actually heard me when I told him I couldn't give him children. I know he only told me he loved me, not that he wanted to marry me or have babies, but it was more than I could handle. I wasn't the type of girl he wanted or needed in his life. I was trouble with a capital T and he knew that the moment he asked me to come home with him. It was all my fault for chasing after Mason in the first place, and that was why I didn't respond to him. Or reach out to him.

I just wished that he tried harder.

Three months. That's how long it had been since I saw those eyes in person or smelled his skin or felt his touch. Missing Mason was something I wasn't afraid to admit.

Tonight Tessa had convinced me to go to the annual carnival in town. She said it was loaded with rides, food, and tons of fun. I wasn't big on the rides or food part, but I was up for the fun thing because didn't everyone want more of that in their life?

After picking out a pair of black skinny jeans and a loose blue sweater, I shoved my feet into a pair of worn sneakers. My hair had started to grow back from the cute little bob that I had had it cut into, and I had almost kept it short, but decided to let it grow back out again. I put on some thick liner, mascara, and light concealer before I headed downstairs to wait for my friend.

"Auntie London, you smell pretty." RJ was sitting at the kitchen table coloring when I walked in.

"Thanks, bub." I ruffled his hair. It was starting to curl a bit like Sully's, but it was dark as night like his father's. "What are you drawing?" I looked down at the picture.

"Daddy's car."

I should have known. This kid was more obsessed with NASCAR than any driver I had met. "Looks nice." I kissed his head. "Are you excited about tonight?" I asked him as Brooklyn came walking into the room. She looked stunning as always, wearing a pair of blue jeans, and one of Rand's shirts that had his sponsor on it. Her dark hair was piled high on her head.

RJ jumped off the chair. "Can we go on the Ferris wheel? Can I have cotton candy?" He was already headed straight for the door.

Brooklyn closed her eyes for a second. She had been looking more exhausted than normal these days and I wondered if taking care of a toddler, her husband, and me was starting to take its toll on her. "I'm going to need so much caffeine to get me through tonight," she muttered as Rand walked in through the front door.

"Give me a second to change." He didn't hesitate to touch Sully's ass as he brushed past her which caused her face to turn pink.

Rand had been working on one of the old cars he had recently purchased. It was something he decided he wanted to do to keep himself busy since he wasn't going to be able to race for the rest of the season. Rand went to some of the races, but most of the weekends he stayed home driving my sister nuts. Sully had told him he needed a hobby because, and I quote, "fucking her every single way he could think of was only going to get them into trouble."

Gross.

"Don't be long!" Sully called after him. "We're supposed to meet everyone there at six." She sat down on one of the kitchen chairs.

Everyone was literally everyone we knew in town. Lake, and a very pregnant Harper, Mia and her twins and, of course, Finn. I thought for sure that they would try to stick Mason in the mix, but his name was never mentioned nor did I see him.

"Knock, knock." Tessa stuck her head in the door.

"Just in time." Rand grabbed his keys from the wall before he scooped RJ up into his arms. "Darlin', you sure you're up for this? We can stay home." He used his other hand to tilt Brooklyn's face up.

"I'm fine," she assured him as she got back to her feet. "Let's go out and have a good time."

———

The drive to the carnival wasn't long, maybe about ten minutes, and before I knew it Rand had parked his SUV in the field across the street so we could head over. I was surprised how many people were already there, but I guess it was a yearly tradition from what the advertisements around town had declared. I could smell the cotton candy, hot dogs, fried dough, and hamburgers before I even saw them.

Harper and Lake were standing by the entrance as we walked up. It was hard not to notice Harper since she was nine months pregnant, although gorgeous as always. Her red hair was piled high on her head in a perfect bun while she was dressed in an amazing green maternity dress that seemed to mold to her body.

"I look like a beached whale." She grunted as she placed her hands on her lower back. "She better come out soon or I'm making her come out. Honestly, why didn't someone warn me that by now none of my shoes would fit, that I wouldn't be able to see my feet or that I wouldn't be able to shave my own snatch?"

"Harper!" Brooklyn covered RJ's ears.

Lake swung his arm over her shoulders. "Freckles, it's alright," he assured her. "We'll find a place to sit down so you can rest. I'll even rub your feet." His eyes shined like the New York skyline when he spoke.

Mia and Finn seemed to arrive at the same time with Noel and Noah. RJ was so excited to see his friends, too. Those three were going to be bad news when they were older. I was convinced something was going on with Mia and Finn, but I hadn't actually voiced my opinion on the matter. I guess it was possible that they were just friends, but the way they looked at one another was something completely different.

"You two don't have to stay with us," Sully said. "Go off, have fun. Just make sure to meet us back here at nine." She smiled.

"What do you want to do first?" Tessa linked her arm through mine. I was getting used to her touchy-feely nature the more we hung out. "You like rides?" She tugged lightly as I stopped to look around.

I shrugged. "Honestly? It doesn't really matter." I didn't actually want to tell Tessa that I hadn't been to one of these before. Back in Connecticut, they had had one in my town, too, but due to my eating disorder I had avoided going. In fact, I had avoided a lot of social engagements with my friends because food was always there and I didn't want to have to deal with it.

Tessa chewed on her bottom lip. "Come on." She started walking, so I had no choice but to follow her. "My favorite ride when I was a kid was the scrambler. So, let's try that." She stopped at the ticket booth and as we waited in line, I glanced around to do a little people watching.

One thing I noticed was the couples. There were couples everywhere. Holding hands, laughing, sharing ice cream, or even a drink. I wondered what it would be like to come here with Mason. Would he do something like this? I shook my head. I had to stop thinking about him. He was not my future, nor had he ever been. Christ, I really needed to get out of North Carolina before I let him consume my life any more than he already had.

"Hey, you alright?" Tessa broke into my thoughts as she held out a ticket for me.

I nodded. "Sure." I smiled. "Let's go check out that ride," I told her.

———

My face hurt from smiling and laughing so much. I was pretty sure that Tessa and I had ridden every single adult ride at the carnival, not to mention she had twisted my arm, well not exactly twisted, and I ate fried dough and half of her caramel apple. I even won one of those stupid little stuffed teddy bears playing a dart game which I planned to give to RJ when I got home so that the twins wouldn't be jealous. I couldn't remember the last time I had that much fun. We were going to meet back up with everyone to head home, and I was honestly sad that the night was over.

"I told you," Tessa gloated as she licked the edge of her ice cream. "You didn't want to come, but it's the best." Her silver hair was a mess from all the wind and rides.

"You're right."

"Wait!" Tessa stopped. "Let me get my phone so I can record you saying that."

We both giggled hysterically as she pretended to stick her phone in my face so she could get me saying that, and that was when I saw them. Mason, Apple and her daughter. Standing by one of the kiddie rides looking like a happy family. Mason was wearing jeans as well as one of his shirts with his sponsor on it that clung to his body perfectly. Apple looked a little less skanky than normal with jeans and a dark sweater, but her jeans were painted on tight. Her blonde hair was tied into a braid that matched Frankie's. I suddenly felt like I was going to be sick as the fun I just had disappeared from my mind.

"London, ignore him. He's a motherfucking bastard." Tessa jumped in front of me after dumping her ice cream in the garbage. "He's a piece of shit. He doesn't deserve you."

That wasn't the truth though, was it? *I* had *left* Mason and told him to find someone else. So why did it hurt so much? I couldn't seem to look away as I watched Frankie holding onto Mason's hand while Apple scrolled through her phone. Tears blurred my vision as I stared and wished I hadn't come tonight.

"There you are!" Rand's voice was in my left ear, but still I couldn't stop staring. "Fuck," he muttered when he realized what was going on. "Shit, that's the kid, isn't it?" I heard him ask.

I suddenly realized what was about to happen. Brooklyn was going to see Frankie and all hell was going to break loose. There was no way she wasn't going to know that was Cooper's daughter. The copper-colored hair, the eyes, that fucking smile. I shook my head as I watched Mason lean down to say something to Frankie, and that's when he noticed me. His eyes went wide, his mouth dropped slightly, and then he was headed right for me.

"Mason? Where are you going?" Apple shook her head as she realized he was coming for me before she took her daughter's hand to keep Frankie from following after him, and watched as he approached me.

I turned to run, but it wasn't fast enough. Mason's arm wrapped around my waist and he pressed his chest against my back. "What the fuck, baby?" His deep voice sent shivers down my spine.

I turned slightly so that I could look up into his eyes that were so dark they looked black. They were mixed with confusion and hurt as they searched my own. "Family fun night?" I asked before I managed to pull out of his grip. "Looks like you're having fun." I put my hands on my hips.

"You know damn well it's not fucking family night, London." Mason's voice was almost a growl. "I've given you the space that you asked for. I didn't expect to see you, but now we're going to fucking talk."

"I don't want to talk to you. If I did, I would have taken your calls or answered your texts." I reminded him.

Mason raised his chin. "Too bad." A smile tugged at his lips.

"You think that this wasn't a setup, London? That no one knew I was going to be here, too?" He let his words sink in.

"Wait, what?" I shook my head. "They wouldn't."

"They would." Mason nodded. "I've been begging your sister for weeks to get us together. I think that Sully finally got sick of listening to me."

My friends and family did this to me? They let me come here knowing that Mason would be even though I didn't want to see or talk to him? People that said they loved me? Cared about me? Anger and humiliation flushed through my body.

"Please, baby. Just listen to me."

"Why don't you go play in traffic?" I pushed at his chest, but Mason didn't move. In fact, he didn't even flinch when I touched him. He grabbed my wrists and pulled me closer.

"I miss you. Don't you understand that?" he whispered. "Why are you making this so difficult?"

"You can't want someone like me. We've gone over this. You need a good girl, with a decent head and not the complications that I come with. I can't give you what you want." I let the tears fall down my cheeks this time because why not?

Mason's hand cupped my cheek. "How do you know what I want? Do you have any idea what it has been like in my head for the past few months? All I do is think about you. I see your face everywhere. I want you!" He rested his other hand on my hip. "You, baby, are *everything* I have ever needed or wanted in my life."

"Let me go, Mason." I shook my head. "That's what you need to do. Let me go and move on." Mason needed to find someone that wouldn't fuck up at the drop of a hat. If he could just understand that he wouldn't be standing here with me right now.

Mason's chin quivered slightly. "Is that what you want, London?" He dropped both hands from my body. I nodded and he straightened his shoulders. "Fine. Consider yourself free."

And just like that, I watched as Mason walked away. Walked over to where Apple was standing talking to my sister. What in the actual fuck? They didn't look to be best friends, but they weren't screaming or pulling each other's hair. Did Sully know about Cooper having a kid? Because right now I was watching my nephew, Mia's twins, and Frankie play together like they did it all the time.

Sully looked over at me the second Mason approached Apple. Then she said something else to her, gave a little wave, and started over my way. "Are you alright?" She pushed a piece of hair behind my ear.

I shook my head. "It hurts so much." I sobbed before I threw myself into my sister's arms.

"Ssshhh." Brooklyn rubbed my back lightly as I cried. I didn't even care who saw me or who might be watching. I was having my heart broken for the first time. Really broken. "Let's go home," she suggested.

I didn't argue. In fact, I didn't even look over at Mason or Apple as we left the carnival. Tessa tried to apologize about what happened. Said she was sorry that she didn't tell me. I don't even remember if I answered her or not.

The only thing I remembered from the ride home was this

announcement from RJ.

"I'm going to marry Frankie," he said it so seriously and not like he was a freaking toddler in blinking sneakers. "I'm going to be a NASCAR driver like daddy and she wants to be a doggie doctor." He looked so proud of himself.

Brooklyn spun around from the front. "Sweetie, you're four. You'll meet plenty of girls or boys before you're ready to settle down," she reminded him.

"No, I love her." RJ shook his head.

This family was seriously fucked-up.

Chapter Fourteen

MASON

I had never experienced heartbreak before and it hurt like fucking hell.

I told myself that I wouldn't be *that* guy. That I wouldn't be that kind of pussy that would hole up in his apartment and be depressed about the fact that his girlfriend dumped him. Although officially London wasn't ever my girlfriend, but it didn't matter. So, instead I decided to put my dick in any fucking chick that would let me as a means to try to forget about her. Not exactly the best plan, but fuck you.

Not my fucking finest hour.

The first race after that disastrous night, I crashed my car eighty-two laps in. Most likely because of the raging hangover that was blaring behind my eyes, but I blamed it more on the sun glare in my eyes instead of owning up to my own problems. I did the usual wave to the crowd after I climbed from my car to let them know I was fine, thank God for all the safety gear, and climbed into the ambulance that was required of me if I couldn't drive my car back to the garage so that I could be checked out to make sure I was okay.

Once I got the A-OK from them it was time to go out to do my post-race interviews. "Mason, what happened out there?" or "Mason, you sure took a hard hit today..." or my favorite "Mason, anything you want to say to your fans or anyone back home that might be watching?"

London Sullivan you ruined my goddamn life was not exactly

the answer I could use so I chose the nicest thing I could think of. "Been having a rough go of it lately, you know how it is, Blake." Blake being Blake Black the reporter. He was a cool dude and I liked him. "Hopefully things will look up. Hate it for the guys back at the shop, hate it for Fahrenheit Games who is my new sponsor, and I hate it for the fans who wanted much more for me today." What the fuck else could I say? Cut to me opening up my Monster Energy, also a sponsor, taking a drink, and tilting my head at the camera. I was very thankful I had my sunglasses on because hatred burned bright behind them.

Once I was finished with all the interviews, I started back to my RV. I knew I had to pack up my shit so I could head on to the next race. This was one of the weeks where I wouldn't be going home, and I was glad. I didn't want to go back to that apartment where London's ghost would be waiting for me around every damn corner.

"Sorry about your car."

I stopped before I even realized it and turned to face the voice that had spoken. Her beauty was intoxicating, a bandage on my wounded soul. Blonde curls that fell in perfect ringlets around her face and down her back. Big, green cat-like eyes that sparkled like candles that watched me with ease as I felt the blood rush to my cock. "It's shit luck, but I wouldn't be here talking to you now would I?" Her skin was kissed by the sun, and my mind traveled south as I followed her curves.

A smile tugged at her heart-shaped lips. "Is that how it works, Mason?" Her voice was sweet, but flirty as she took a step closer. "You think you can charm your way into my panties by saying things like that?" She pressed the palm of her hand against her heart. "What makes you think I'm *that* type of girl?"

"Wouldn't be talking to me if you weren't, would you, sweetheart?"

We barely made it back to my RV before my fire suit was around my knees, her mouth around my cock, and my hands wrapped in her hair. Sweet little thing knew how to suck a mean cock, too, because I was blowing my load down her throat in no time. She took it like a champ, purring and sucking it all down.

"You don't think that's all I have for you?" I struggled out of my clothes before I brought her up to her feet. "Sweet little thing like you, giving me head like that deserves something in return." I ran my tongue over the seam of her lips before I plunged inside.

Her eyes went wide before she sucked hard on it and wrapped her arms around my back. Her nails dug deep into my skin as I palmed her round ass and lifted her up onto the table. "Fuck me." Her breathy voice whispered when I pulled back.

"That's the plan, sweetheart." I unbuttoned her shorts before I slipped them down her legs. "What's your name?" I hadn't even asked her before I let her suck my dick. Off came her little white panties and I stepped back to admire her glistening mound.

"Hanna." She watched as I moved between her legs, and she widened them without hesitation. She inched herself closer to the edge of the table while I slipped a condom over my shaft.

"You ready to come for me, Hanna?" I pressed the head against her slick entrance. I didn't wait for her answer and thrust inside. I watched as her mouth fell open, her hips jerked up and a cry of pleasure tumbled from her mouth.

"Shit," Hanna whimpered as I gripped her hips. Her pussy clamped down tight on my cock. Her eyes rolled slightly as I kept moving. My balls slammed against her ass as I fucked her harder, faster, plowing deep inside her.

I hooked my arms underneath Hanna's frame and lifted her up before I pressed her against the wall. Her cries of pleasure had turned into breathy moans as she gripped me like a vise. She pulsed and rippled around me as I continued to try to fuck London out of my memory. Hanna tugged at my hair as beads of sweat slicked down my back.

Hanna's orgasm was wild and ripped through her, followed by another. She buried her face into my neck as a fireball of bliss began to travel up my spine. The need to explode built inside me and I moved hard in my desperate attempt to reach my climax. It almost felt violent when I finally did explode inside the condom, the tendons on my neck tight from gritting my teeth so hard.

"Jesus Christ." Hanna brushed the damp hair from her forehead once I placed her onto her feet. "Is it always like that?" She reached for her panties on the floor. "I've never had a guy fuck me like that." She wiggled them up over her hips.

"You can go now." I didn't even want to look at her. I felt ashamed of what I just did and she should, too. The sound of the door slamming shut told me Hanna was gone before I had to ask her to leave again.

That's how it pretty much went after that. I would fuck any

girl that looked at me. One, two, three at a time. I just didn't give a shit. I started sharing girls with Watson Brooks because no one else was fucking interested, and I was fucking desperate. I needed to get her out of my head and what was better than a kinky-ass girl?

Except, I *couldn't* get London out of my brain. I saw her when I went to bed. I saw her face whenever I stuck my dick in some random pussy. When I came, I saw the way she looked when she came. I heard her moan when it should have been someone else. I was addicted to London, and I needed to find the cure.

"Thanks, Mason." Ava the slender brunette kissed my cheek lightly as she picked up her purse. "That was the best sex I've had in a long time." She turned to look at Watson, who was still lying on the bed. "You, too, handsome." She wiggled three fingers at him.

"Babe, any fucking time," he called back. "Next time we come to race here you know I'll call you."

Bullshit. He didn't even put Ava's number in his phone. Just all nines which is a trick I fucking taught him.

Ava brushed her dark hair from her shoulder. "Sounds like a plan." She blew him a kiss. "Bye, fellas." Once she was gone I turned to face Watson as he pulled his jeans up. Seeing him naked didn't bother me, but I think he was still getting used to seeing my cock.

"You're getting pretty good at lying to them." I tucked my shirt into my pants.

Watson chuckled. "What can I say, man? I had a good

teacher." He pulled open the fridge door. "You want a beer?" He glanced over at me before he reached inside.

I shook my head. "Thanks, but I'm going to head back to my place and try to get some rest." Which was code for me to drink myself into a fucking stupor before I passed out so that I could get up, race, and go home where I hated to be these days.

With a casual fist bump, I left Watson's place, I pulled out my cell ignoring the missed calls and texts to see that it was nearly midnight as I headed into the cool, dark evening. Nights like this made me wish I was already cuddled up in my bed with London wrapped around me, but I pushed that thought out of my head. It wasn't going to fucking happen because she *told* me it wasn't going to happen.

"Christ, dude, have you been ignoring us or what?" Finn's voice caused me to nearly trip over my own feet.

"Sorry, I've been balls deep in some chick for the past couple of hours" I rolled my neck as I felt his icy demeanor "What's up?" I glanced behind him to see Lake and Rand standing there. Well, this is going to go fucking swimmingly.

Rand bared his teeth. "What's up?" He growled at me. "Well, clearly we should have staged some sort of fucking intervention for you." He suddenly looked larger than life.

"Go fuck yourselves." I started walking again, but felt a hand on my arm. "If you don't want to lose those fingers, I would let go." I didn't know who it was, but I didn't care.

"You're out of control, Pelletier." Lake walked around me so that he could see my face. "Fucking anything that walks, drinking too much. Don't think we don't see that."

I gave him a lazy smile. "Look at you, mister fucking perfect. You're sober for a few years, get married, have a kid, and what? You're the king of everything? Not everyone can be as wonderful as the royal Lake Mills." I shrugged off the hand on my arm before I made sure to smack into Lake as I brushed by him.

"Mason—"

I spun back around. "No, you fucking don't." I pointed a finger at Finn. "You're fucking a woman whose husband hasn't been in the ground for—"

The fist that hit me sent me flying back. I tried to catch myself, but the whiskey from earlier was still swimming through my bloodstream, and I threw my arms out in some sort of pinwheel motion despite the fact I *knew* I was going down.

"Shut the fuck up!" Rand's face appeared before my eyes as I blinked up at him. "You're acting like a fucking child right now." His voice was loud enough to wake the dead. "Get your fucking shit together because this has nothing to do with you anymore." His eyes had turned to angry stones. "Why are you doing this? Why aren't you fighting for her instead of doing... whatever the fuck you think you're doing?" Rand's nose twitched with hate. "If you weren't my best friend, I would fucking beat the shit out of you."

Lake touched his arm. "Don't wake everyone up." His voice was oddly soothing.

I scooted myself up into a sitting position as I glanced between the three of them. "What aren't you telling me?" When no one responded I ran my hands through my hair.

Rand squatted down. "What do you think, dick?" He leaned

so close that I wanted to joke about him buying me a drink before he kissed me, but I didn't dare. I knew before Rand said it what was about to come out of his mouth. "It's London."

My heart was in my throat, but I pretended not to care. "So?" I shrugged as I struggled to get back on my feet. "Which one of you assholes hit me?" This time I saw the hand that was coming toward me. The one that grabbed my throat and pushed me back against the tree.

"So?" A terrible hatred spilled from Rand's body. "You have two fucking seconds—"

"Dude." Finn reached for the hand that was around my neck. "Easy." He pushed Rand out of the way. "She's sick, Mason. She's in the hospital again, and we need your help."

"London doesn't fucking want me," I reminded the three of them. "She fucking told me to let her go."

"She almost died."

Rand's cruel words felt like bullets in my heart and the loneliness that suddenly hit me felt like a lightning strike. "Where is she?" I whispered as I realized I almost lost the woman I loved because I was a fucking idiot.

Forever.

"She's in the hospital, but we should talk about what happened first," Rand told me. "You can't just barge right in there, man."

"Fuck that, London is mine and I will fight every fucker that tells me otherwise. I need to see her. I'm going to save her." The words tumbled from my mouth. It didn't matter that it had been nearly a year since I saw her or spoke to her because I hadn't stopped loving her. I never would.

"Alright, let's go talk about this," Lake suggested as a couple of lights flicked on in the RV next to where we stood. "Where we won't wake anyone," he added.

I followed the three of them back to my RV as I started to think about how I would save London. I would climb that castle wall for my woman, slay the monsters, and be her knight in shining whatever.

Chapter Fifteen

London

At first I sunk into the deepest depression that I had ever felt before. I stayed in my room for days on end, sleeping, crying, and doing nothing else. I didn't shower, I didn't eat, and that was when my anorexia came back and it came back with a vengeance. It happened so fast, I wasn't sure that anyone was even aware of it.

Harper gave birth to her first child a week after the carnival. Kayla Grace Mill came out with a full head of beautiful blonde hair like Lake, and gray eyes, like her mother. I guess she was seven pounds, eight ounces, but I didn't pay too much attention to that. The whole baby thing made me realize if I was ever lucky enough to find someone else that wanted me? I wouldn't be able to give him a son to name junior or a daughter to name after his great aunt on his mother's side.

I was fucking useless and hated myself for it.

One night Brooklyn found me in my bathroom sitting on the floor with a razor blade in one hand and Mason's spare key in the other. I couldn't remember the last time I had left my room, spoken to my friends or eaten anything other than a handful of crackers that I kept under my bed. The food my sister brought to my room for breakfast, lunch, and dinner got thrown into a garbage bag that I kept hidden in the closet which I'm sure she's already found by now.

Sully didn't say anything as she walked into the room. I'm sure she was horrified at the sight of me, the smell even, but instead she got onto the floor and maneuvered her way next to me. I'm sure it wasn't easy with her being four months pregnant.

That's right, Rand and Brooklyn were expecting again.

"Talk to me, London." Sully pushed the unwashed hair from my head as she leaned hers against mine. "What's going through your brain right now?" I let her take the razor from my hand, but refused to give up the key.

I felt the flower of shame as it began to bloom inside me. "I'm sorry," I whispered as a sob threatened to escape my throat. "I didn't... it just..." I buried my face against my sister's chest.

Brooklyn let me cry until I felt like I had nothing left inside me. The fear of what was to come knotted inside my gut. She didn't tell me I told you so or I knew you would end up hurt. "I love you, you know that, right?" She cupped my face in her hands. "You're so smart, so beautiful, and I wish you could see that. I wish you would tell me what happened to make you like this." Her brown eyes filled with tears. "I would do *anything* to take this away from you." Brooklyn pressed her lips to my forehead.

A wave of apprehension washed over my body. Telling Sully about Cooper was my worst fear. It would make her hate me. "Don't cry. I don't want you to feel like this is your fault." I chickened out.

"I know, Lon." She sighed. "You've been holding onto that key since he left it, huh?" She flashed a quick smile.

"It makes me feel better."

"You still love Mason."

I wanted to withdraw at the mention of his name. "Please..."

I shook my head.

Brooklyn nodded before she put her arm over my shoulders. "You know you're going to have to get some help for this. Finding you sitting here with a razor blade, not eating, not bathing... it doesn't look good."

Desperate tears spilled over my cheeks. "Please, I don't want to do that again." The thought of going back into the hospital was worse than anything. "I promise I'll eat, and I'll—" One look at my sister told me this was a fight that I wouldn't win. That I *couldn't* win no matter what. I hung my head in defeat.

Thirty minutes later Brooklyn was driving me to Carolina House, an eating disorder treatment center.

———

It could have been worse. This place wasn't as bad as some of the places I had heard about. I could have pretended it was a retreat of some sort if I didn't have to get weighed every day, talk to a shrink and have group therapy. Of course there were arts and crafts, but I had time to write songs if I wanted.

In the beginning, I didn't want to talk to too many people. I did what I was supposed to do, ate when they told me and helped cook the meals like I was supposed to. I kind of liked that part. I had never really been big into cooking before, but here they were teaching us how to cook healthy meals with vegetables. Not just dinner, but breakfast and lunch, too. It would be nice to be able to make something other than boxed mac and cheese for RJ when I got home. I told my therapist that, too.

"You like cooking?" Diane, everyone liked to go by their first name here, asked as she typed something into her laptop. "Maybe it's something you can look into when you go home. Maybe go to school."

Not happening.

I shook my head. "I like cooking, but I'm a songwriter," I told her. "I'm going to go to Nashville someday." I picked at the dirt under my fingernails.

Diane nodded. "You could probably do that here." Click, click. She typed more into her computer. "Tell me more about your home situation, London. You live with your sister and brother-in-law. Do you like it there? Do you have a boyfriend or girlfriend?" She smiled at me. She was pretty with streaks of gray in her dark hair.

"It's alright." I looked out the window as some of the others strolled around the grounds. "I'm single." I didn't want to talk about Mason, but I knew this conversation was going to go there.

"Your sister mentioned..."

"We broke up," I snapped. "Sorry, I didn't mean... shit." I pressed the palm of my hand to my forehead. "I was after him for a long time."

Diane tilted her head. "When you say after him, what does that mean?" She crossed her feet at the ankles.

"I met him for the first time when I was a kid. Around thirteen, I think. He was nice to me, he saved me once and I sort of started crushing on him. When the situation presented itself..." I let my voice fade off.

"When the situation presented itself, what?" Diane was typing again, and it took all I had not to fling that computer across the room.

"We fucked, okay? At a friend's wedding. It wasn't supposed to be a forever thing, but then he stepped in and saved me when I had a party after Brooklyn freaked out. I stayed with him for a few days. I guess I fell in love or whatever." I didn't realize I was crying until the tears landed on my hands. Shit.

"And, do you think that he fell in love, too?" Diane closed her laptop, and I found her smile comforting.

I nodded.

"But, you broke up? Did you break up with him or did he break up with you?" When I didn't answer Diane folded her hands over the laptop. "When you say he saved you..."

"I told him he had to let me go. I'm not good enough for him. I can't give him anything he would want. I can't have babies. I'm ruined. I'm tarnished and tainted. Cooper made damn sure of that." I clapped my hand over my mouth as I realized what I just said.

Fuck, fuck, fuck!

Diane's eyebrows went up. "Cooper? Is he the one that said you weren't good enough, London?" The laptop was open again, her nails clicking the keys echoing through my ears. "Was he a boy you knew? Dated or maybe went to school with?" Again, I didn't answer. I didn't want to talk about him. Cooper didn't belong in my life anymore, yet I couldn't seem to forget him.

"London, you're not going to get better if you don't let it out. Whatever it is. This is only between you and me. No one else. I won't tell your sister or brother-in-law and there's the whole patient-doctor confidentiality thing." She drew her eyebrows together.

I wrapped my arms around myself as I shook my head. "I don't... Cooper was Brooklyn's... please don't make me." My voice shook as I spoke.

"Did he hurt you?" Diane put the computer down on the chair next to her before she got up to move onto the couch next to me. I cringed at the thought of her touching me, but she didn't try. "Did Cooper force himself on you?" Diane smelled like strawberries. How weird that I would notice that right now.

"More than once."

"Sweetie, did you ever tell anyone? A friend maybe or an adult?"

I brought my eyes up to Diane's. "He was Brooklyn's boyfriend. He was the poster boy for racing, and...I couldn't tell anyone because..." A terrible laugh burst from my chest. "No one would have believed me if I did." I jerked away from her touch. "Please, don't," I warned her.

Diane let out a shaky breath as her timer went off. "Shit." She glanced over at me. "Sorry, I just wish we had more time." She went back over to her chair. "I want to see you again tomorrow instead of waiting until Friday." She scribbled something down on a piece of paper. "Sweetie, the more you talk about it, the better you're going to feel. I promise."

Spoiler alert. I didn't.

I wasn't allowed to have my phone, use a computer or see anyone other than family at the treatment center. There was no television or magazines. There were some books that were approved by the medical staff and anything that was brought in from the outside had to be preapproved as well.

I missed the shit out of texting, but found I didn't really miss social media all that much after a couple of days.

Sully came to see me every other day. She would talk to me first, then go talk to the doctors before she said goodbye. It was nice to see my sister when she came, but she didn't need to visit so much. It was the day that Rand showed up alone that shocked me the most.

I was sitting outside reading Harry Potter when I heard my name. I glanced up to see my brother-in-law standing there, looking smaller than I thought possible. "Is Brooklyn okay?" I asked as he sat down next to me.

Rand ran his hand through his hair before he spoke. "Are you getting better?" He answered my question with a question.

"Is this about the money? Because—"

"Fuck the money, London. I don't give two shits about how much it costs." He turned his body to face mine. "Are you getting better?"

Did Rand care about me or did Sully send him here? I had been here nearly a month now, but this was the first time he had come to visit. I shrugged. "I guess." I sat back on the swing.

"Can you talk to me about what happened?" Rand leaned closer.

I lowered my gaze and pulled my legs up underneath my body. "I'd rather not." I pulled at the hem of my pants.

"What about me, baby?"

I froze at the sound of Mason's voice. What was he doing here? How did he get in and why was he here? My eyes went to Rand first who was already on his feet so that Mason could take his place next to me. All I could do was stare at him, afraid that if I blinked, he would disappear.

Mason's fingers grazed my cheek as he lifted my face up. "I'm sorry." His voice was barely a whisper. "I'm such an asshole for not fighting harder for you, London." He ran his thumb over my bottom lip. "I knew what happened, what he did, and yet..." He rested his forehead against mine.

"I told you to let me go, Mason. You were only doing what I asked." I swallowed my fear as I stared into his chestnut brown eyes. "If you had stayed, I only would have pushed you away harder." I reached up to grip his shoulders with my hands.

"You should have called me. London, when Rand told me you were sick again..." Mason shook his head. "I wanted to storm the castle to save you." His fingers were in my hair. "I want to spend forever saving you, baby." Those lips of his were so close I could kiss them.

"Mason—"

"Don't say anything." Mason stopped me. "Don't say yes, don't say no." He began to fumble in his pocket before he removed a small box.

"Don't you dare." I shoved off the seat. "This isn't a damn pity party. I'm not doing this because I want attention because you, of all people, know that's not what I want." I held my head up as I watched Mason's reaction.

"Do you know what I went through while we were apart?" Mason remained seated. "I drank every night until I blacked out. I would wake up with raging hangovers in the morning, but that didn't make me stop. I hardly finished a fucking race because my brain couldn't function right knowing you were out there alone, and the worst part? I stuck my dick inside anyone that would let me." The look on my face must have been pure disgust because Mason shook his head. "I hated myself. I saw you *everywhere*. Your voice, your laugh, your eyes. I couldn't get you out of my fucking mind, and no matter who was wrapped around my dick, I only wanted you, London. I picture *your* pretty little cunt as I fucked some random girl in Texas. It was *your* mouth on my cock when I was in Talladega, and it was *your* voice screaming my name whenever I made that girl come. *You*. You're the only girl for me."

He fucked other girls. He probably fucked a lot of other girls. Bile filled my throat at the thought of Mason touching someone else or kissing them. *You did that, London. You told him to leave, to find someone else. You can't get mad.*

"Baby, those girls meant nothing." Mason had opened the box in his hand and inside was a beautiful diamond ring with two-toned gold wrapped around what looked like a rose. "It's a special edition." His cheeks were red with embarrassment. "It's a Disney collection or something they told me.”

“Beauty and the Beast,” I murmured.

Mason nodded. “I thought it would be perfect because, you know, because I want to be your Prince Charming. You don’t like it, do you? I can get you something else. Maybe you don’t like diamonds.” He closed the box.

“Mason.”

“I should have thought about that before I bought it. Maybe asked Sully, but I wanted to make it a surprise.”

“Mason!” I grabbed his hand and he stopped to stare at me. “Ask me.”

He looked confused for a second before a sly smile tugged at his lips. “London Sullivan.” Mason dropped to one knee. “Will you marry me?”

Chapter Sixteen

London

In my mind, I said yes. I wanted to tell Mason I would marry him so we could spend the rest of our lives together. Except, I *couldn't* do that. I couldn't say anything to Mason at that point because what was going on wasn't real.

I made it up inside my head.

Sully didn't find me that night when I was inside the bathroom with my knees tucked up to my chin, shaking and sobbing about how much I hated myself. Hated what I had become and what I had done to my family, my friends. I wish she had because I wouldn't be where I am right now.

I opened my eyes and let them adjust to the lights overhead. Bright, horrible... hospital lights! I sat up so fast the heart rate monitor attached to my body sounded like it just went into overtime. The familiar NG tube in my nose to force-feed me some high calorie supplement didn't upset me as I resisted the urge to rip the IV from my arm as realization set in.

I had attempted suicide and failed. Christ, I couldn't even do that right.

I heard the whispered sound of slippers as another patient walked by my room with their IV beside them. Sitting outside the door was a tray of food that clearly wasn't for me, but the smell of burned, overcooked toast filled my nose. I lifted my hand to brush my hair from my face and the sight of the bandage wrapped around my wrist nearly made me scream.

Jesus, how long had I been here? Where was *here* exactly,

and the thought made me shiver as I wondered who found me that night?

"Holy shit." Mason's voice caught me off guard as I turned to see him stumbling up off of two chairs he had pulled together to, maybe, sleep on. "You're awake. I should get someone." He started toward the door, but stopped to look at me. He walked back over to me. "Why?"

I stared up at him. "Why what?" I knew what Mason was asking. I wanted him to actually ask me.

"Don't fucking..." He closed his eyes and I watched as his nostrils flared while he tried to gather his thoughts together. "If you had died that night, I wouldn't be able to live with myself." His brown eyes were swimming with so many emotions when he opened them again.

"Bullshit."

Mason flinched. "You have no fucking clue how much I love you, do you? Or your family? What if it was RJ that found you? You would have ruined that boy for life." His body stiffened. "I know that I don't know what you were going through or feeling, baby, but you have got to start talking to people. To me, or Sully or that friend Tessa of yours." Mason pinched the bridge of his nose.

"Who found me?" I asked curiously.

"What the fuck, London? Haven't you been listening to me?" Mason roared and I was sure that someone would come in to save me. To find out why someone was yelling so loud in the middle of my hospital room. The anger in his eyes was enough to make me realize he was serious. The days of stubble that covered his face, the wrinkled clothes that looked like he had been sleeping in them for weeks. "You were lying in a pool of your own..." Mason had started to pace the floor, but at that moment a nurse came into the room.

"You were supposed to tell us when she woke up." The pretty brunette glared at Mason before she got to my side. "I'm going to get a doctor to check you over." She was punching numbers into her computer that she had rolled in with her. "Do you remember what happened?"

Her badge read Annie, and as she fussed over me I kept my eyes on Mason. He had moved as far away from me, and the nurse, as possible, but his eyes never left me. "No, not really," I answered truthfully.

Annie's eyes flicked over to Mason before they moved back to me. "Your brother-in-law found you on the bathroom floor after you sliced open your wrists." Her lips twitched. "The right way, as you kids might say."

Mason's eyes widened. "Annie," he warned.

"I know, Mason." She turned slightly and that's when I saw it. The baby bump hidden underneath peach-colored scrubs. "If this is a problem for you, you can always wait outside." She winked at me as she checked my fluids.

"Miss Sullivan!" A tall, blonde doctor wearing wire-rim glasses that for some reason reminded me a little bit of John Lennon. "I'm Dr. Ackerman." He was looking at what I assumed was my chart. "I'm sure Mr. Pelletier is happy to see you're up and awake. He's been sleeping here for two days."

Two days?

"I've been here for two days?"

"Three days actually." Brooklyn answered from the doorway. Rand was right behind her, and I watched as he wrapped an arm around her waist to put a hand possessively on her stomach. She was really pregnant. That part I didn't make up. Christ, these pregnant women made me thankful I couldn't give birth because clearly something was in the water right now in North Carolina.

"I'll let you talk with your family, but not too long." Dr. Ackerman nodded. "We have a lot of things to discuss about your future, young lady."

I wanted to like him, but I always hated my doctors when I was in the hospital. The therapists, the nutritionists, it didn't matter. They all taught me things I already knew, yet I couldn't seem to comprehend.

Annie had stopped right next to Mason and as she looked up at him with big, doe eyes. I resisted the urge to scream at her. He wasn't mine anymore. He never had been. "Call me," she mouthed before she patted her stomach.

No.

"Get out," I demanded when we made eye contact. "Get the fuck out of my room." I grabbed the empty Styrofoam cup sitting on the over the bed table to throw at him, but it landed on the floor next to me without much success.

"It's not what you think, baby." Mason held up his hands.

Rand suddenly blocked my view. "Let's go get something to eat." He told his friend. "Let them talk first, and we'll come back." He was already guiding Mason from the room.

"Don't bother to bring him back!" I called after Rand as my

sister sat down on one of the visitors' chairs.

"You could have told me." She had her hands in her lap. "If I had known he did that to you, London, I would have broken up with him. He was scum anyway, and for some unknown reason I was the only person who couldn't see that."

My blood roared in my head. "Who told you about that?" I needed to get out of here. "The only other person who knew… I'll kill him." I flung the blanket off my legs only to be reminded I was in nothing but a flimsy hospital gown.

Brooklyn touched my hand. "Don't be mad at him. He loves you, Lon, and wanted to help. Mason thought that if he told me about what happened with Cooper, it might help me understand things a bit more." Her lips formed a thin line. "I'm so sorry," she whispered.

"It's not your fault."

"I brought the wolf into our home, London. I trusted him to be a good person when he was wearing nothing but sheep's clothing."

I saw the pained look in Brooklyn's face, and I didn't want her to feel what she was feeling. Not now nor ever. She didn't do anything wrong. "He let you believe he was a good person, Sully. He tricked you just like he tricked the others." I took her hand.

"Like Apple." The way her name sounded on Sully's lips told me she still didn't trust her. "He lied to her, too. Told her they were going to get married, have a future together, and yet I was the one with the ring on my finger. How many others did he tell that to? Or how many other girls did he hurt like he hurt you?" Brooklyn squeezed my hand. "I wish that I had never met

Cooper Houston." Her voice was cold when she spoke.

I bowed my head and looked at our hands intertwined. My sister. My best friend. How could I have kept this secret from Brooklyn for so long? All she ever wanted was the best for me from the day our mother dropped me at our grandparents' house. All I ever wanted was to be as good as she was, but right now I realized we were both pretty fucked-up even if all of my scars weren't on the outside.

Sully tugged on my hand. "You're going to get better. We're going to do this together, do you understand?" Tears swam in her eyes. "Whatever we have to do… because I believe in you."

Shit, she was really laying it on thick today.

I nodded. "Okay." I flashed a quick smile before I saw movement out of the corner of my eye. Rand was in the doorway, holding a cup of coffee in one hand and a white paper bag in the other. "I'm sorry." I blurted out when I met his gaze.

Rand moved closer. "You have nothing to apologize for." He handed the bag to Sully before he put the cup down. "I consider you to be my little sister, too." He grinned when I let out a small laugh.

"We're two years apart, asshat."

"Doesn't matter. I'm bigger."

I didn't deserve them. I was the jerk that didn't tell her sister that her boyfriend raped her, took her virginity, and yet here they were. They loved me, cared about me, and I realized how fucked-up I had made everything.

"We'll let you two have some time to talk." Rand held out his hand to Brooklyn who took it happily.

I didn't realize Mason had come back into the room either. I narrowed my eyes. "I have nothing to say to Mason." I refused to look at him again.

"Tough shit, baby." Mason sat down in the chair that Brooklyn just vacated. "You have to listen to me."

"I don't." I crossed my arms over my chest.

"That isn't my fucking kid."

My eyes flicked over to Mason for a second before I went back to staring at the wall. "Don't believe you," I muttered. I let out a squeal of surprise when Mason climbed up into the bed. My heart began to beat faster than ever as I felt him press every inch of his body against mine.

"She's a fucking liar, London. Think about it. How long ago did I have sex with her? The timeline isn't even right. She was clearly pregnant before she fucked me." His breath was hot as his hand turned my face so that I had no choice but to look at him. "I wore a condom, and," Mason growled softly. "I didn't even fucking come. I tried, but she didn't do anything for me. All I saw was your fucking face." He pushed my legs open with his knee. "Do you understand me?"

I licked my lips before Mason's mouth swooped in to steal a kiss. But it wasn't stealing if I wanted it, was it? The kiss began to set fire to my entire body as I realized that his mouth wasn't flirting, but demanding. I laced my fingers through Mason's hair as his probing tongue danced against mine, and I suddenly realized I was tasting salty tears.

"Mason." I cupped his head in my hands. I brushed the wetness from his face.

"I should have done more." He pulled away from me to sit up. "I should have said something to Sully back then, but I was too chickenshit. I was too afraid that I would get kicked out of the boys' club, and I wouldn't have a shot at doing what I loved." He pounded his fist against his thigh.

"Mason."

"Maybe you wouldn't have tried... maybe you wouldn't be..." A sob burst from his chest as he stood up. "You deserve better than me."

What was going on right now? Didn't Mason just spend two nights sleeping in the hospital to prove to me we should be together? Didn't he just assure me that he didn't impregnate that cunty nurse?

"Why? Why me, London?" Mason demanded. "It could have been any driver, but you picked me. Why?"

"You saved me," I reminded him. "After that night, the one where you stopped Cooper, he never touched me again. You were always kind to me when you didn't need to be, and you continue to be that way. Even now." I patted the bed, hoping he would sit back down.

Mason eased himself onto the mattress. "So, does that mean we're back together?" A smile pulled at his lips.

"We were never together, Mason," I reminded him.

"But, we are now." He held up his hand. "We have a lot to figure out, but I want you. I love you. You were built for me, baby."

I thought back to the dreams I had. The ones where Mason admitted to fucking every single woman he could, and I wondered if it wasn't exactly a dream, but him confessing to me. "Did you talk to me when I was out of it? Because—"

"You heard what I said." Mason tilted his head to look at me. "Yes, I did talk to you. I had to get everything off my chest because I felt so fucking guilty. I should have chased you down instead of letting you go."

"I love you."

Mason's eyes lit up. "Yeah?" He twisted to face me.

I nodded. "Pretty sure I've loved you since I was a kid, but it took you awhile to catch up," I teased.

"We're going to make this work," Mason assured me. "Everything is going to work out for us, you'll see, baby." He leaned in to pull me against his chest.

Chapter Seventeen

It would be two months before London would be able to come home with me.

First, she had to be discharged from the hospital and then she had to do some inpatient therapy for her eating disorder as well as her suicide attempt. It was hard not to see her every day because goddamn, I wanted to be with her. I knew that London wanted to get better. I knew she needed to do it alone.

I visited her every Wednesday before I left for the race. And, when the end of the season came, I was able to stay close by so that I could visit every single day. We talked about our future, we talked about buying a house, and we talked about what she wanted to do with herself when she came home with me.

Home. I wanted to provide London a better one when she returned, but I wanted her help in picking it out. It was funny to me that the guy who never wanted that shit, the house or the garage, was now planning on buying one.

"What kind of houses do you like?" I sat across from London one evening after we had finished eating dinner. I was literally counting down the days until she was released. Not only did I miss her, but my hand wasn't cutting it anymore.

She wrinkled her nose. "What? I don't really care." London tilted her head. "That's kind of a strange question." She stretched her legs out and nudged my feet with hers.

"It's not if I want to *buy* you one, baby."

London's mouth fell open. "Don't." She shook her head.

"Mason, your apartment—"

"Is too small, not a home for us, and I want to buy you the fucking world." I got up and moved around the table so that I could sit back down. I pulled her into my lap even though I knew it was against the rules. "I can't wait to get you home." I kissed her softly.

"You're not buying me a house." London narrowed her eyes, but a smile tugged at her pink lips. "But, I like the one Rand has. You know the whole wrap-around porch thing is kind of nice." She giggled as the nurse reminded us that we were too close, no touching, and that it was almost time for me to leave.

That happened a lot when I was here.

I let my fingers trace her lips. "So, you want something like Shepard's?" I could do that. I'd seen something similar when I was driving around. "Maybe with a big room to write your music in?" I smiled against her hair as the nurse hollered at us again.

All too soon I had to say goodbye, but at least I knew now what kind of house I could look for. I stumbled across the perfect place a week later. At first it was the damn porch that made me stop to look, but maybe it was the granite countertops or the actual fucking pantry that made me realize *this* was the house I wanted to live in. This house with the gas fireplace, the French doors, two walls of windows in the Livingroom, and the trey ceilings in the giant master bedroom, I had to look those up to find out it makes it look like a higher, second ceiling above it, but it's the fucking bomb. There were three bathrooms, including one for us in the master, and three extra rooms so we could have a couple guest rooms as well as a room for London to work.

It had a two-stall garage too which was perfect since I didn't have a million cars like Shepard, and I loved the pale yellow color.

I offered to buy it the second my tour was done.

"Well, do you want to put in an offer?" the realtor asked.

"No, ma'am, I want to buy it. I have the money," I assured her.

"Buy it? Outright?" Her face paled.

I nodded. "Cashier's check."

"Holy shit."

I liked this chick.

I picked London up at the hospital two days later with the key to our new house in my hand. I hadn't told her yet because it was just one of the surprises I had planned. The other one was tucked under the passenger's seat that my girl had just sat her beautiful self in.

"Check under your seat, baby," I instructed as London started to pull on her seatbelt. She stopped to look at me.

"Why? Is there a snake under there or something?" A smile tugged at her lips.

I shrugged. "Guess you'll just have to look and see." I climbed into the car as she scooted back out.

London leaned down as she pressed her hand underneath. "What is this, Pelletier? A game? Because I'm not really a fan of surprises." Her fingers made contact with the papers I had stuck there because I heard the sound. London's blue eyes narrowed as she dragged them out from beneath the seat. "Seriously, what..." Her voice trailed off as she realized what it was. "Plane tickets?"

"Yes."

"Las Vegas?"

I nodded. "Are you up for a trip?" She looked at me curiously. "Feel like getting hitched?"

London threw herself into the car so that she could climb up onto my lap. "Are you fucking serious?" she whispered before she slid her lips across mine.

"Why wait, baby? I want you to be my wife. Now, forever and always." I gripped her thighs as she straddled my waist. "I booked us a chapel, a hotel room, and there is *nothing* keeping us from doing this except you. Say yes." I silently begged London not to say no.

"Sully—"

"She knows. I already told your sister my plan," I assured my soon-to-be wife, but didn't tell her that Brooklyn and Rand would be meeting us there for the wedding. That was part of the surprise, too. "You're it for me, London." I reached up to run my hands through her hair that had grown back. "I think I might have realized it the first time I saved you, but you are fucking *it* for me." I pushed my chest against hers.

"Mason...."

"Let me finish, baby." I placed my finger over her lips. "Deep down I knew there was something special about you the first time we met at that race. I was too busy chasing after long legs, big tits, and all the pussy I could get, but I saw you." Jealousy flashed in London's eyes, which made my cock jump just a bit between my legs. I loved how fiercely she loved me. "You were a shy little girl just standing there with your sister and... him." I hated to say Cooper's name. "But, you watched me with eyes full of curiosity, and so, I watched you back. I knew the age difference would be a problem, so I didn't say anything."

London moved so that our noses were touching. "You shouldn't have waited, Mason." Her mouth brushed mine. "Let's go get married." She smiled shyly at me before I crushed my lips against hers so hard I thought I might bruise them.

When we finally broke apart London was smiling. "Let's get moving." She cupped my face in her hands before she scurried off my lap to get back into her seat. "I've never been to Las Vegas before," she confessed once we both buckled ourselves in.

"Just wait, baby." I reached for her hand. "You're going to have so much fun."

London squeezed my hand tightly. "We're getting married," she whispered.

Yes, yes, we were. And I was about to claim this woman as mine.

———

The moment the plane landed in Las Vegas, my stomach was in knots. No, it wasn't because I didn't want to get married. It was because I was afraid that London would change her mind about marrying me. I wasn't perfect. I had made a lot of mistakes, but I wanted to fix this one. I should have saved her years ago when I realized she was the girl for me.

"You alright?" London bounced on the heels of her feet as we waited for our luggage.

"Yes."

She looked up at me. "Are you getting cold feet on me, Pelletier? Because if you've changed your mind or don't want to do this? We can go right now." Her body language said that was fine, but her eyes? Her eyes said something completely different.

"Baby." I stepped forward to wrap my arms around London's small frame. "I most certainly have *not* changed my mind, nor have I gotten cold feet," I assured her as I slid my lips against hers.

London giggled as she buried her face against my chest. She was like a child seeing Disneyland for the first time as we rode to the hotel, turning her head to try to catch everything.

"We have time to take a trip to sightsee," I assured my bride to be as the Uber pulled up in front of our hotel.

London opened her mouth to answer me, but gasped instead when she saw the place in front of us. I had booked a luxury suite at The Venetian which I had hoped that she would love and clearly, by the look on her face, she did. It came complete with a king-size bed, a sunken living room, a roman soaking tub, and a separate glass shower that I could hardly wait to fuck my girl in.

"Looks nice, right?" I hooked my arm around her shoulders.

"This... this is too much." London wheezed as we stepped into the lobby.

I smirked. "You don't want to stay here? Would you rather

stay at the Circus because I heard they might have some rooms available?" I roared with laughter when she slapped at my chest playfully. I loved to see the happiness in her eyes and the smile on her face.

"Mason, what am I going to get married in?" London asked as we waited in the elevator. "I didn't bring anything fancy and I don't want to wear a pair of jeans." She leaned into me.

"What about this?"

Yet another surprise for my girl as she turned to see her sister, Brooklyn, standing there with her husband, my best friend, Rand Shepard. Rand was holding what I assumed was the dress in a garment bag. London flew at her sister and hugged her tightly as Shepard and I bumped fists before he rolled his eyes to pull me into a half hug.

"Feels a little familiar," he joked. "I mean, you're not asking me to bring you a tux."

"Got that all set." He was talking about when he married, which was also a spur of the moment thing after his accident in Charlotte. Rand had decided he didn't want to wait anymore and married her in the hospital with a bunch of friends and family around.

Rand pursed his lips while he nodded. "Seems that you got it all figured out, man, I'm proud of you." He leaned closer. "Lake wanted me to tell you that he told you so and when he sees you again, he'll make sure to remind you he was right."

Dick.

The girls had stopped their tears and gabbing so we finally managed to get onto the elevator as I noticed that RJ wasn't around. "Where's the boy?" I asked.

"With Harper and Lake," Brooklyn answered. "We decided we would have a little babymoon before this one came along." She ran her hand over the swell of her stomach.

"That sounds nice." London lifted my arm and put it around her shoulders. "Are you going to tell us if that's a boy or a girl?"

"No," Rand and Sully both answered at the same time.

"Fine." London stuck out her tongue as the elevator stopped.

Brooklyn stepped forward. "Do you, uh, mind if I spend a little time with my sister before you two get hitched? I mean, after you get settled in your room? It's bad luck to see the bride on your wedding day anyway." She looked up at Rand who had touched her shoulder.

"Sure, just give us a few minutes," I assured her. "Or maybe like an hour." I wanted to have my way with London first. It had been a while.

"First off, gross," Brooklyn teased as they stepped off the elevator. "Lon, text me," she called as the doors closed.

London turned around to look at me with hooded eyes. "Just an hour?" She slipped her hands up my chest.

"I'm going to tie you to the bed, baby." I groaned as she pressed her small body against me. "Do you know how many nights I've thought about you? My fist doesn't compare to that pink little pussy of yours." I tugged on London's bottom lip with my teeth before she opened her mouth to me.

"Show me," London cooed softly as I picked her up so she could wrap her legs around my waist.

The moment those doors opened to our room, perks of

having the penthouse, I had London's back pressed against the glass, her pants around her ankles, and my dick inside her while she clawed at my back screaming my name.

I could already tell I was going to be married.

Chapter Eighteen

London

I brought my hand up to my hair and lightly touched the flowers as I stared at myself in the mirror of the chapel Mason had gotten for our wedding today. I liked them much better than a veil. I just didn't think that was me.

Holy crap! I was marrying Mason Pelletier in less than ten minutes.

The dress that Brooklyn had lent me looked perfect. She had it taken in in all the right places so it fit. I didn't have her chest or her curves, but for once in my life, I actually *liked* the way I looked when I saw my reflection. I even let Sully do my makeup, too, because why not? It wasn't the heavy eyeliner look that I usually went with, but it was light and flirty which didn't look too bad either.

I was getting married!

"You holding up alright?" Sully smiled at me when I met her eyes in the mirror. "You look beautiful. Mason is going to melt when he sees you."

I swallowed the lump in my throat. "I can't believe… this is so crazy." I turned to face my sister. "All these years, I had a crush on him." I blushed.

"All these years I thought he was such a dirtbag."

"People change," I reminded her, and I wasn't just talking about Mason.

Sully nodded. "I'm so proud of you, little sister. You're going to make an amazing wife, songwriter, and someday, a mom. I hope that you know you can adopt when the two of you are ready. If you want to have a family. I don't want you to think I'm being pushy." She touched my cheek lightly with her hand.

The doors behind us suddenly burst open and Rand rushed inside. His eyes darted over to my sister, to me and back to Sully again. "Can we talk, darlin'?" He sounded nervous.

Brooklyn took a step forward, but I stopped her. "What's going on?" I raised my eyebrows.

"What? Nothing," Rand assured me, but his face said something completely different.

"Shepard, you have two seconds to talk before I make you." Which I couldn't or wouldn't, but still. I folded my arms over my chest without thinking about the fact I would probably wrinkle the dress.

"Mason's gone."

My stomach dropped and I reached for the wall because I suddenly felt like I might pass out. "What do you mean he's gone?" I exclaimed as I stared up at my brother-in-law. "Gone from where? The chapel? Maybe he needed to take a walk." That was probably it. He was nervous. I was nervous, too. I understood that—

"Gone, London. He left. I went up to the room to get him, and..." Rand held out an envelope with my name on it. "I found this."

I grabbed it from him to rip it open and as I began to read I felt myself sink to the floor.

I'm sorry.

That was it? Just a fucking note with two words on it that

told me nothing! I resisted the urge to rip it into a million pieces. I wanted to set it on fire while I screamed, yelled, and stabbed Mason Pelletier in the heart. Except this time the tears wouldn't flow, my voice wouldn't come, and I had nothing to hurt him with because he had hurt me with something much worse. Empty promises.

"London?" Sully had knelt down in front of me. "What does it say?" She touched my face.

"I'm sorry."

Brooklyn looked up at Rand as he punched the wall so hard his fist went right through it. "I will kill him," he exclaimed. "Fucker can pay for that, too, since this is on his credit card." He rubbed his knuckles.

"Lon—"

I jumped up. "No, I'm done with feeling sorry for myself. I am done with Mason, too. Whatever excuse he comes up with? I don't want to hear it." I looked between the two of them. "Let's get out of here," I suggested.

"But, Auntie London, I thought you were going to marry Uncle Mason?" RJ blinked up at me with big eyes. "Why are you sleeping in your room? Shouldn't you be sleeping with him like Mommy and Daddy sleep together?"

Why did kids have to ask so many questions?

"Hey, bud, you want some ice cream?" Rand to the rescue.

Again.

I gave him a half-smile as he placed a bowl of strawberry-flavored sweetness in front of my nephew. Sully had gone to bed after we returned from picking up RJ. She was exhausted from the flying and because of the pregnancy. Rand placed a bowl in front of me, too.

"Thanks," I said softly.

He nodded before he scooped himself some and sat down at the table. No one said anything as we ate our frozen treat, but my heart was heavy. My head was full of the promises and lies Mason had filled it with.

"Don't do that." Rand shook his head when I lifted my eyes up. "You didn't do anything wrong. This was all him, and when I find out what happened—"

"Fuck him," I blurted out without caring about my nephew. His little eyes went wide. "I know, the swear jar." I held up my hand before RJ could remind me. "He did whatever he did because he pussied out, Shepard, and I am *done* with him." I took a bite of my ice cream. "I'm not going to wallow in self-pity again. He's not worth it," I went on. "I'm through with Mason because he's just going to hurt me again and again. I'm not going to do that to myself anymore." Although I had thought he was my happily ever after, but clearly he didn't feel the same.

"You sure?" Rand asked. "Because I was pretty sure the two of you were written in the stars."

"Not anymore." I finished my dessert and stood up to put my bowl in the sink. "Thanks, Rand. I mean it. You're pretty awesome. Too bad you couldn't clone yourself," I teased.

He snorted with laughter. "Too bad my brother is an A.S.S.H.O.L.E." He spelled it out for me so RJ couldn't understand, but the way his little eyebrows shot up I wondered if he figured it out on his own. "The two of you might have hit it off." Rand didn't talk about Eli often, but I knew deep down he missed him.

"I'm going to go unpack." I gave him a quick hug before I dropped a kiss on RJ's head and I hurried up to my room. I pushed the door open and stepped inside.

Everything was just as I had left it. My notebooks were piled high on the desk in the corner while the basket of clean clothes still sat on my unmade bed. The hamper was full of dirty clothes, and I wondered how badly they were going to stink when I got around to washing them. I wasn't sure how long I stood there before I took a deep breath to move inside.

I opened the window first before I dumped the clean clothes onto my bed. Next, I took all the dirty clothes from the hamper and ran back down the stairs to start a load of laundry. Rand and RJ were sitting in the living room now with some Disney movie on. I think it was *Cars* but I wasn't sure. Once the washing machine was started I went back up to my room, folded my clothes and put them away. Then I opened up my suitcase.

The new notebooks that Sully had provided me went onto my desk and as I started to pull out the dirty clothes, something fell on the floor. As I leaned down to pick it up, I realized it was Mason's key. The key that I had used as an anchor of sorts. I stared at it for a few minutes before I stuck it in my underwear drawer without giving it a second thought.

Then I went back to emptying out the rest of my suitcase.

I slowly began to let myself have a life here in North Carolina.

I started seeing a new therapist twice a week and a nutritionist that helped me with making sure I was not only eating enough food, but how to make sure I was eating enough protein, fat, vegetables, and carbohydrates. I no longer wanted to go back to Connecticut, but knew it would soon be time to find my own apartment and go out on my own.

I hadn't spoken to Mason since he left me at the altar, but Rand had. I wasn't privy to the exact conversation, but apparently it had something to do with Annie, the nurse he swore he didn't impregnate. Turns out it was in fact his kid, they had bought a house together and were living there now.

I wanted to hate him, but I didn't. Mason had done a lot for me, even if he did end up breaking my heart in the end. He had been my knight when I needed him, and almost my Prince Charming.

Brooklyn refused to speak to him and didn't want him in our house, but she had started letting RJ and Frankie have playdates together. Yes, that meant she was speaking with Apple. Turns out that she had found out about Apple having Cooper's baby before the night of the Carnival, so that's why she didn't totally freak out or lose her mind when she saw Frankie. Sully told me she would never be best friends with Apple, but hoped that Finn might be able to have some sort of relationship with his niece, and, when Apple was ready, maybe Frankie could meet her grandparents.

"So, what? You just kind of stand here to see if he walks by?" I whispered to Tessa as we stood at the end of the hallway of the motel she worked slash lived in.

Tess rolled her eyes. "Duh, that's the whole idea. He's hard to catch sometimes because he gets up super early for work, so he's probably super important. Like a lawyer." She brought her hands up in front of her and gripped them together.

"Or a thief," I muttered under my breath. I didn't think that a lawyer would live in this dump, but I kept that part to myself.

"I heard that."

I giggled. "Why don't you just go talk to the guy?" I asked. "He's not going to fucking bite you unless you want him to." I watched the blush creep up Tessa's neck. "Just go pretend you need to clean his room or something."

Tessa sighed. "Like I haven't thought of that before." She let her shoulders slump forward.

"Just fucking go do it," I urged her. "If he doesn't open the door at least you can say you tried."

Tessa nodded before she moved to grip the handle of her cleaning cart and wheeled down the hall to stop in front of the guy's room. She knocked on the door, but when there wasn't an answer, she tried again. "Housekeeping." She used her fake customer service voice as she leaned her head against the door. Her eyes swiveled over to meet mine and I waved my hands at her to go inside. Tessa then used her keycard to open the door and slip on in.

I stood there waiting for my best friend for what seemed like forever. Since I had started working Tess and I didn't get to spend as much time together as we would like. Texting was pretty much the only form of communication unless we were lucky enough to share a day off which was unlikely. My phone buzzed in my pocket and I took it out to see a text from Sully.

My sister was so pregnant right now. Like nine months, beached whale, get this thing out of my vagina because I'm over it already pregnant. She wanted me to bring home more Cherry Garcia ice cream. Again. I swear that Sully ate at least two pints of this stuff a night. I looked up from my phone the same time as the door to the mystery guy's room opened expecting to see a very disappointed Tessa, but that was not the case.

"See ya around, sweetness," he called over his shoulder before he started to walk toward me. His eyes met mine for a brief second before he winked, flashed me a quick smile and moved on his way. I started to follow him because I could have sworn that that had been Rand who just walked down the dirty hall and left the faint smell of cigarettes behind.

The height wasn't exactly right and his dark hair had been a little shorter than Rand usually kept his. But the eyes were spot on. Blue as the morning sky, and shoulders made for a football player instead of a NASCAR driver.

"London!" Tessa was suddenly gripping my arm so tight I thought she would cut off the circulation. "Did you see him? Wasn't he like the hottest guy? He was wearing a fucking towel when I walked in!"

I met her eyes. "Did you get his name?" I asked.

"What? No, but did you see him?"

"Tess." I removed her vise-like grip from my arm. "Did you notice anything about that guy that looked, I don't know, a little familiar?"

She shook her head. "Nope." She made sure to let the p pop at the end. "Why, should I? Do you know him? Shit, if you know him—"

"I think that's Rand's brother."

Tessa's mouth clamped shut for about two point two seconds. "Rand has a brother? Can you introduce me to him? How did I not know he had a brother? Where has he been hiding?" The rest of her questions turned into white noise as I started to wonder if I was actually right.

Did Rand know Eli was back? Would he *want* to know he was back? Should I tell him Eli was back? What the hell was going on right now?

"Hey, are you listening to me?" Tessa waved a hand in front of my face.

I moved my eyes back to my friend. "This is a problem." I chewed on my bottom lip before I spoke again. "Eli and Rand... they aren't exactly speaking." I wouldn't say anything else about their relationship. It wasn't my business.

"Oh."

Oh, shit was more like it, but I didn't say that out loud. "I should go. I have to pick some ice cream up for Sully on my way home. We're still on for tonight, right?" We both lucked out to have tonight off, so we were doing a girls' night at my place.

Tessa threw her arms around me. "Of course! I've been looking forward to this all damn week." She squeezed me tightly before she pulled back.

"See you tonight." I smiled before I started my car and climbed inside.

<u>Chapter Nineteen</u>

Mason

I stared down at the baby who was staring up at me with big, brown eyes. If you didn't know any better, you would probably think that this was my fucking kid. Dark hair, dark eyes... you get it.

Parker was not my child.

I hated myself for what I did to London. I hated Annie for making me do this. I hated what she was doing to this poor child because he was innocent in all of this. His real father, whoever that was, deserved to know Parker existed so that he could be a part of his life.

"Babe." Annie's voice was like nails on a chalkboard as she called out to me from the other room.

I closed my eyes for a second before they popped open again. "What do you think, pal?" I tickled Parker's little belly and he gurgled at me. "Do you think people are buying this bullshit or do you think they can see through it?"

Parker gave me one of his gummy smiles as he kicked his feet up into the air.

"Mason!"

"Fuck," I groaned, not caring that I was swearing in front of the kid. Not my problem if he turned out like me. Annie knew what she was getting into when she roped me into this farce. "Come on." I scooped Parker up into my arms before I went to find out what his mother needed.

Annie was spread out in the middle of my bed, although I

refused to sleep with the sea witch, with the covers wrapped around her. "My boys!" she cried out when I walked into the room. Her inky black hair was a mass of twists and curls falling down her back.

"Only one," I reminded her before I handed her son over. "I'm not your anything."

Annie puckered her lips up and pushed them to the side. "You sure about that?" She dropped a couple of fingers against Parker's little belly. "If you want me to call your—"

"Stop it, Annie. You've done enough damage already by bringing that man back into my life. Lying and convincing him I should be with you instead of the woman I love." I felt my blood begin to boil at the thought of how she roped me into this by going to my grandfather, of *all* people.

Annie bounced Parker quietly before she spoke again. "You deserve so much more than her, Mason." She refused to even say London's name around me, and I felt the jealousy as it burned from her body. "She's crazy, messed up, and can't give you the babies you deserve." Annie kissed Parker's face.

I clenched my hands into fists. "You spied on me. You blackmailed me so that you could get what you wanted, Annie, and I will never give you what you want. You can live in my house, pretend that child is mine, but you won't have my kids. I'll have a vasectomy before I let that happen." I stomped off into the bathroom before I made a mistake and said anything else.

I turned on the shower after locking the bathroom door behind me so Annie couldn't accidentally walk in on me. That was something she loved to do back at the house. Walk in on me when I was changing or at least naked claiming it wasn't on purpose, but I could tell she was lying. Her cheeks would flush, her lips would purse as she blinked those big doe eyes like she was so innocent.

"Bullshit." I turned the water on as hot as it would go and began washing up for the day. I hated being here without London. I wanted to bring her to every single race with me, but that would never happen. Not now with what Annie had done.

London. Just thinking about how I had promised her forever and then left her like that made me hurt all over. I tried to ask Shepard about her, but he refused to answer me. In fact, he hardly spoke to me at all these days along with Finn and Lake. I was pretty much outcast from that group of friends, but I could hardly blame them for that. Rand had to side with his wife, just like Lake, and Finn would never cross Sully either.

Once I was done with my shower, I stepped into the small bathroom to wrap a towel around my waist. I looked and felt like shit. I wasn't eating right, I wasn't sleeping much, and I was miserable. I had no one to talk to and there was more than one occasion that I turned to the bottle, but I couldn't do that. I had stopped drinking with the help of Lake, and even though he hated me now I didn't want to disappoint him.

I ran my hands through my hair before I went back into the bedroom. Annie was no longer on the bed, so I assumed she was feeding Parker. I dressed as quickly as I could before I grabbed my phone and started to leave.

"You need to make sure we're at the race tomorrow." Annie

was sitting at the kitchen table with a bottle stuck in Parker's mouth. "Henry isn't going to like it if he doesn't see your fiancée and child there."

I grimaced at the sound of my grandfather's first name. How did she even find out who he was? I wondered. "You can be there, but don't expect me to like it." I slammed the door on my way out without caring if it bothered the baby.

When I got that call from Henry, that fucking asshole, I was in the middle of putting on my suit for my wedding. I hadn't spoken to him in so long that it scared me to see his number come up on my phone. I thought maybe he was hurt or sick, so I answered. I wish that I hadn't.

"Son, you need to stop this wedding."

Not even a hello or hey, Mason. That was how he greeted me when I answered.

"What?" I was confused as to how he even knew where I was or what I was doing.

"That girl," Henry roared into the phone. "She's trash, Mason. She's not the one you should be marrying nor is she the one carrying your son."

"How dare—"

"Spare me," Henry cut me off. "I know you impregnated that nurse and tried to tell her you didn't. I saw… well, let me just say that I saw the video of the two of you together so clearly—" He paused. "You need to start thinking about your future, boy, because if you want me to keep sponsoring your car so you can keep racing—"

"I love her, Gramps." I wasn't afraid to tell Henry how I felt about London. I assumed that he must have been in love once when he was younger.

Henry chuckled. "If you really love her, then you'll forget about her before her life is ruined because you decided to stick your dick in someone without protection."

Annie had taped us having sex. It was my own fault for going to her place instead of insisting we meet up at a hotel, but I was trying to prove I didn't have a thing for London that night. I still hadn't found out how she knew about my grandfather or gotten in touch with him, but it wasn't a secret that he was my main sponsor in NASCAR. He had paid for me to go through school, helped me with my career and never let me forget it. It was Henry threatening to expose London's secrets that made me realize I had to protect her. I would *always* protect her.

I sighed as I got closer to the track. Racing just wasn't any fun for me anymore. Not now that I had to bring that woman with me and pretend that I wasn't miserable. That we were one big happy fucking family.

I made my way over to my car and wondered how long I would be able to pull this charade off. I watched Rand and Finn as they talked together just as I felt a hand on my shoulder.

"For the record, I'm not mad at you." Lake's eyebrows shot up when I turned to face him. "I'm just trying not to upset my wife." His lips twitched as if he was trying to hide a smile.

"Figured as much."

"Look." Lake turned over his shoulder to glance at Rand before he spoke again. "If you knocked up this chick, and you feel this is the right thing to do, that is a pretty noble thing. But, and this is a pretty big fucking but, I don't believe it."

"Fine, don't believe me. I don't really care what you, Shepard or fucking Houston think." I hated having to lie to my friends like this. I knew how protective Rand had become of London, like she was his real sister.

Lake held up his hands, palms out. "Easy, tiger. You need a friend right now whether you want to think you do or not." I wondered if he could feel the daggers Finn and Rand were shooting into his back right now.

"They'll stop talking to you."

"No, they won't."

"Your wife will cut your balls off."

Lake flashed a quick smile as he stifled a laugh that threatened to escape. "I'm not as whipped as the three of you think that I am, but that's a story for another time. Look, Mason, I knew you were in love with London Sullivan before you did. It was obvious there was something special between the two of you, but if you're sure you're happy with the nurse, don't worry about us. It's Brooklyn you'll have to convince to forgive you."

"I am happy." I gritted my teeth as I pushed the lie from my mouth.

Lake's eyes narrowed. "Liar." Without another word, he turned and walked away.

Fuck. Fuck. Triple fuck.

After the race—I finished tenth—I hopped on a plane to head back to California. It was an idea that started forming inside my brain while we were under caution around lap fifty-six. I thought if maybe I went and spoke with my grandfather in person, he might realize how terrible this idea was. That Annie was a liar, that she was blackmailing both of us, and that London was perfect for me. Perfect for the family.

Perfect in every way imaginable.

Annie had a million questions. Where was I going, who was I going to see, why couldn't she come, and I just kept ignoring them. I told her it was a work thing, but she could take Parker home where I would join them in a day or two. Hopefully when I did, I could kick her ass out.

As I pulled the rental car down the long gravel driveway to the house where I spent my teenage years, it didn't feel like coming home. This place was never my home, more like a house that I went to when I wasn't at school, racing or chasing tail. The place I was forced to move to when my mother got sick, the place my mother died in, and the place I swore I would never come back to when I left at eighteen. Guess that makes me a liar.

I climbed from the car and removed my sunglasses to get a good look at the house. It hadn't changed much from when I left although the siding was new, and the windows might have been replaced. The stump that once belonged to a tree I used to use to sneak out at night was still there as a brutal reminder of how angry Gramps had been when he found me coming home one morning after not caring what I did for months after my mother died. So angry in fact that he made me cut down the tree with an ax even though there was a perfectly good chainsaw in the shed out back. So angry that he locked and barred the windows in my room, not caring that I could die there if there was a fire.

The man was a fucking bastard.

I walked up the steps and rang the bell, wondering if I should have called first. Henry hated when people dropped by without notice. He wasn't big on friends or parties or interacting with people in general. I often wondered how he met my grandmother or how they had managed to have a wedding with people there to congratulate him, dance with or be near him.

"Well, this is a surprise." Henry Pelletier opened the door before I could ring the bell again. He smirked as he took me in, and I did the same. Just like the house, he looked exactly as I remembered. Gray hair kept close-cropped, thick eyebrows that covered brown eyes that matched my own, and hardly any wrinkles on his sixty-whatever-year-old face.

"May I come in?"

Henry nodded before he turned to go back inside and so I followed behind, hoping that I could fix this. Fix it, make it right, and get my girl back.

Chapter Twenty

London

I waited a week before I said something to Brooklyn about the guy I ran into at the motel. I wasn't sure if it was Eli or not and so before I opened my mouth I snuck downstairs into the storage room to where I knew Rand had hidden a bunch of his stuff. In one of the boxes I found a bunch of old photo albums and began to go through them.

It was Eli alright. I could tell by the nose, the mouth, and of course, those eyes. Eli Shepard wasn't as big as his little brother, but he was still just as good looking. Rand was huge, a giant standing at six foot five, but Eli looked like he was probably around six feet now. At one point he had been the bigger of the two, but it was clear Rand had worked hard to make changes.

There were a lot of pictures of them as babies, as kids, and as teenagers. There were some pictures where it was obvious that Eli was high or shying away so you couldn't see his face. Photographs of them standing outside a run-down RV, others with their arms around each other with huge, happy grins on their faces. It was clear to me that the Shepard brothers had been close, but Eli had an addiction problem that ruined that.

Why was he here now?

"London, what are you doing going through Rand's things?"

I jumped at the sound of my sister's voice. She was leaning casually in the doorway with her dark hair pulled back in a high ponytail and dressed in a pair of black maternity pants with a matching shirt.

"I met Eli the other day," I blurted out before I could stop myself.

"You what?" Brooklyn stepped into the room. "Eli? Rand's brother?" Her face had grown pale. "Fuck me."

"Are you going to give birth right now because I don't want to have to see your lady bits." I jumped up to go to her side.

Sully shook her head. "Where did you see him?" she asked. "You know what? Let's just go upstairs to talk so I can sit down. My feet are killing me."

Her feet were the size of watermelons, but I wasn't about to say that out loud. So instead I boxed back up the albums I had found before I went up to talk to my sister.

Brooklyn was sitting in the living room with her feet resting on the coffee table. "So?" She tilted her head as she waited for me to start talking.

"I was with Tess, you know she works at that dumpy little motel?" I sat down on the edge of the loveseat as Sully nodded. "Eli was there. I wasn't exactly sure if it was actually him or not so I had to look at some pictures. He doesn't know who I am and I was only there because Tessa has been chasing him for weeks."

"Weeks? He's been here for weeks?" Sully cried before she threw her head against the back of the couch. "Rand is going to flip his fucking lid when he finds out."

I wrinkled my face up. "Are you going to tell him? I mean, that I knew Eli was here and didn't tell him?" I didn't want to upset Rand knowing what a hard childhood he had and how badly his brother had hurt him.

Sully waved her hand. "No, no, I'm not going to do that. I'm going to go talk to him first and tell him to stay the fuck away from my family."

"Um, Sully, you're not exactly in the right kind of shape for that. Maybe after you drop that womb troll from your body you can go chasing him out of town." I pointed to her ever-growing stomach.

Brooklyn snorted with laughter. "Womb troll? That's a good one, Lon. I wish she would vacate my body so I can get some sleep." The second she realized what she had said, her hand slapped over her mouth. "Shit, I was almost home free."

"It's a girl?"

"It's a girl."

I was having a niece. "Rand is going to break any guy's face that tries to date his daughter," I teased. "He's going to keep her locked in her room until she's fifty," I added the more I thought about it.

"You're not kidding." Sully smiled. "Can you do me a favor?" She leaned forward, or at least as forward as she could. "Let's just keep this between the two of us for now. He's already upset with Mason, we have a baby on the way and I don't want to add anything else into the mix. We won't mention Eli or the fact that he's back until we can figure out why. Maybe you can have Tessa find out if she gets the chance to talk to him again."

That sounded like a terrible idea, but okay.

"Sure, if that's what you think we should do. You don't think that..." The sound of the garage door opening caused me to stop which meant that Rand was home and we needed to change the subject.

"Thanks, Lon." Brooklyn started to stand up. "Hopefully this won't turn into some giant mess."

———————

It turned into a giant fucking mess when Eli showed up at the house two nights later.

I was sitting on the front porch working on some new music when I saw the car pull up. At first I thought it was Sully's client. Her last client before she went on maternity leave for a few months because the baby was due next week. As I got ready to tell him to go around the side of the house, the front door opened and Sully stepped outside.

"Are you Gary? I'm sorry the sign was knocked down to show you where my studio is, but—" Brooklyn stopped. "You're not Gary."

"No, ma'am. I'm not Gary." Eli squared his shoulders as he looked between me and my sister.

"Rand is going to freak out."

Eli let a smile slip up his face, but it disappeared just as fast as it appeared. "He told you about me?" He looked like he was trying to see around Sully probably to see if Rand was there before he glanced at me again. "Do I know you from somewhere?"

Brooklyn moved the door behind her. "Rand tells me everything. Eli. What do you want?" She folded her arms over her chest as I stood up. I needed to stop this before it got out of hand. Before Rand showed up and really blew everything out of proportion.

"Darlin'? Everything alright?"

Spoke too damn soon.

Sully and I both knew what was about to happen now as Rand appeared behind his wife. He put his hands on her shoulders almost possessively and the moment he saw his brother standing there, his eyes went hard as stone.

"No."

"Hello, little brother."

"Brooklyn, London, get inside the house. Go upstairs with RJ and lock the door. I'm about to fuck shit up." Rand's teeth were clenched together and I saw a vein throbbing in his neck. He looked ready to explode he was so mad.

"Rand." Brooklyn turned around to face her husband. "You have to relax."

"Darlin'."

I put my hands on my hips as I stood there wondering what I should do. If things got really bad I knew Rand would need some sort of help. He couldn't fight his brother on his own if it got that bad. But maybe it wouldn't come to blows between them and they would actually talk it out. Fat chance, knowing him, which meant Eli was probably the exact same.

"Rand Shepard." Brooklyn placed her small hands against his broad chest. "Do *not* kill your brother. Find out what he wants and then send him on his way. We both know he's not welcome here." She glanced over her shoulder at Eli with fire in her eyes. "You need to make this quick because we don't need or want you here."

"Ouch, you don't even know me sweetness." Eli held up his hands when Rand pushed the screen door open. "Sorry, don't forget your wife is pregnant, brother!" He nearly fell down the steps as Rand took a step toward him.

Rand put up two fingers. "Two minutes, Eli. Two fucking minutes and then you leave," he growled angrily.

"Sure, fine. I'm clean and I have been for a couple of years." Eli glanced at me and Sully before he looked back at Rand. "I've been back here in North Carolina for a while, but your friend there..." He pointed at me before he went on. "You might already know that because she saw me at the motel I've been staying at." Rand's head whipped around to stare at me.

You fucking asshole.

"Oh, and Brian gave me a job."

Rand's head swung back around. "Brian did what?" he roared as he clenched his hands into fists.

"He gave me—"

"I heard what you said!" Rand's nostrils flared. "I swear to fucking God you had better not be driving." He glanced up at the sky. "Do you know how much I fucking hate you?"

"You did good with her little brother."

Rand's eyes were black with hate when he looked at Eli again. "You *do not* get to say a word about my wife or my family. Brooklyn is my whole world and without her... you know what?" He shook his head. "Fuck you, Eli. Your two minutes are up." He turned to stomp back up to the house.

"Great catching up, brother," Eli called out to him. "I'll see you at work," he added, which only made Rand shoot up the middle finger.

"In the house, London," Rand hissed at me. "Because we clearly need to talk."

I gathered up my notebooks to follow behind him.

"When and where did you see him? Why didn't you tell me about this?" Rand demanded the second I stepped inside the kitchen. "What the fuck, London?" His eyes were no longer angry, more like hurt.

"I... I wasn't sure it was him, and I didn't want to upset you," I muttered softly.

"Rand!" Sully exclaimed. "Don't talk to her like that. I'm sure that's why she didn't tell you because you'd start acting like a giant fucking asshole. You can't get mad at her for keeping this from you. I told her not to tell you."

"You what?"

Sully put her hand on his arm. "I didn't want to upset you. With the baby coming, this whole thing with Mason... I know how badly Eli hurt you." She stepped closer to her husband.

I took this as my cue to leave the room. This no longer concerned me because I knew how this would end. The two of them would fight or maybe not, but it was time I thought about getting my own place so they could have their privacy. So they could fuck on their kitchen counter if that's what they wanted to do.

In my room, I changed into my pajamas before I climbed onto my bed. Then I had an idea and sent a text off to Tess.

London: *You want to get an apartment together?*

A few seconds later, she replied.

Tessa: *Yes! That would be so damn perfect. I could maybe even leave one of my shitty jobs although I wouldn't get to see that hunky guy every morning.*

I smiled. I'm sure wherever we lived it would be a dump, but it would be a start, and it would be *our* dump.

London: *Awesome, we should start looking ASAP.*

We made plans to meet for lunch tomorrow to talk more about it and then I went to bed. Hopefully it wouldn't be long before I could be on my own, with my best friend and maybe after that I could start selling my songs.

My future was starting to feel pretty good.

Chapter Twenty-One

MASON

I slipped into the booth across from Apple and met her blue eyes. "What?" I asked as she raised her eyebrows.

"Nothing, boo, but you look like shit." She smirked her red lips. "It's nice to finally see you again. How come the ball and chain let you out?" Apple reached for the water in front of her.

"She thinks I'm at work."

Apple nearly spit the water out of her nose. "You're lying to her already?" She blotted her mouth with a napkin and I noticed the lipstick stain she left behind. "Mason, honestly, leave the bitch because we both know how miserable you are. You were so much happier with London. I know something isn't right here." She touched my hand, but I jerked away. "Well, fine." She folded her arms across her chest.

"I'm sorry, Apple, but you don't know shit." I grabbed the menu and started to flip through it. My visit with Henry had gone as terrible as I thought it would and I left with him telling me if I didn't stay with Annie he would not only have *me* fired, he would have Lake fired, too, and he would make sure everyone knew about London's suicide attempt.

Fucking Annie told him all about how she ended up in the hospital and apparently didn't give a flying fuck about hospital policy or HIPAA or losing her nursing license. Bitch was crazy, but I only cared about trying to protect London.

The waitress came over to take our orders and when she left, I looked up to face Apple again.

"I'm sorry, look, there's a lot you don't know about and I can't tell you. You know I would, but not now. How's the kid?" I knew Frankie had been spending time at Shepard's place which I found interesting, but left that part out.

Apple smiled. "Frankie's good. She loves school and spending time with RJ. Insists they're going to…" Her voice trailed off as her eyes zoomed in on something behind me.

I turned to see what she was looking at and felt my stomach drop when I saw it was London waiting to be seated with her friend Tessa. She looked beautiful dressed in a pair of blue jeans and a sweater that clung to her in the right places. Her dark hair had grown out from when she had it cut and I loved the messy bun thing she had pulled it up in. I spun back around to face Apple before London saw me.

"It's only a matter of time before she notices me and realizes that I'm here with you, Mason," Apple whispered. "One, two, and it's done."

"Really?" I asked as I felt London next to me before I looked up. The scent of the body lotion she always wore filled my nose, replacing the smell of grease from the restaurant. Gone was the usual thick eyeliner I was used to seeing, but instead she looked fresh-faced, and even more beautiful than ever before. The hate I expected to see wasn't there, and I realized all I wanted to do was kiss her lips, tell her I loved her, and fix this whole fucking mess.

"Hello, Mason." London nodded at me. "Apple." She didn't leave my best friend out either.

"It's good to see you, bab… London." I felt like I couldn't

breathe right now. "How are you?"

London shrugged. "Pretty good considering what you did. I have a job now." She avoided my eyes by staring at my nose. "I just thought I should say hi because, you know, you were here and all. I didn't want to make things awkward."

I wasn't sure how it happened, but I stood up and grabbed her before she could go. "I'm sorry, London. You know I would never hurt you." I needed her to know that.

"You've said that before."

The urge to kiss her was overwhelming, but I couldn't do it. If I did it, London could lose everything and I couldn't do that to her. "You look beautiful," I whispered before I let go of her to sit back down.

London hurried off without another word and when I looked at Apple again her eyes blazed with anger.

"Go get her. I don't want to hear any excuse about Annie or some kid that we both know isn't yours, Mason. You love London. She loves you. I've never seen you act that way with any other girl," she told me.

I shook my head. "I can't." I sighed. "If I do... never mind."

Apple kicked my shin. "If you don't tell me what the fuck is going on, boo, I am walking out of this restaurant. Do you understand? We tell each other everything," she reminded me.

I needed to tell someone what was going on. It would at least make me feel better to get it off my chest. So, I told Apple everything. About Annie, my grandfather, and how Parker wasn't mine.

"You're not staying with that crazy bitch another night. I'll go there myself and drag her out by her hair."

"You can't—"

"I can and I will! That's against the law what she did, Mason!" Apple exclaimed, ducking her head as people turned to look at her. She continued with her voice at a lower level. "She can't just release London's medical information like that. And if your grandfather fires you, someone else will hire you. The same with Lake because hell, he's a NASCAR champion. He'll have to justify the firing first, and how exactly can he do that? Huh? Think about it."

I shook my head. "I don't care about my job, but Lake is my friend." Neither one of us had touched our food.

"You can't let them push you around like that." Annie sipped her water again. "You did it to protect your girl, your friends... you're a good guy, Mason."

"Why don't I feel like a good guy? I feel like a complete asshole."

"Because you miss London. You miss your friends who are angry about what happened because they don't understand why you left her like that. When they find out the truth, they won't be so upset with you." Apple reached for my hand. "We're going to tell them the truth. You're going to get your girlfriend back, and you're going to get that crazy Annie put in jail for what she did."

"I feel bad for her kid." I squeezed her hand. "Parker's just a baby, and innocent in all of this."

Apple squeezed my hand back. "Do you know who his real father is?" she asked.

My eyebrows dipped down. "I haven't a clue because Annie

won't tell me a thing about him because, of course, she claims I'm the father."

Apple waved the waitress over. "Can we get our food to go instead?" She stood up. "Come on, boo, we're going to get your girl back."

———

Apple followed me back to my place. She had been there only twice before because Annie was insanely jealous of our friendship. Even more than London had been. Annie was home, as she always was, because she only left the house when she had to. I think she was afraid if she left when I was gone, I might change the locks. Believe me, the thought had crossed my mind more than once.

"You stay here," Apple instructed as we walked through the front door. "I'm going to have a few words with her."

"Do you think that's a good idea?"

Apple's lips twitched into a smile. "It's a great idea. I've been wanting to give her a piece of my mind for months now." She patted my shoulder before she headed up the stairs.

I paced the living room floor as I waited. I knew that all hell was about to break loose in my house in three, two...

"Get the fuck out of my house!"

Oh, Annie, you are not going to win this one.

"Do you think it's such a good idea to talk like that around your son?" Apple's voice was coated with sugar and sarcasm.

Ha, like she cared about swearing in front of her own daughter.

Something smashed against the floor. "Fuck you, bitch! Who let you in? Is Mason here? Mason!" Annie screamed so loud I thought she would wake the dead.

"Relax, sweetie. Don't you think it's time the two of us got to know one another? You're dating my best friend, you're the mother of his son… we should be besties, too, right?"

Damn, Apple was good at being bitchy. I just wondered if Annie would play dirty or back down?

"I'll call the police," Annie threatened.

"You think that's a good idea? I mean, with the lies, the secrets, and oh, the fact that you went to Mason's grandfather with private medical information about London Sullivan? That's right, bitch, he told me everything because Mason trusts me."

Something else hit the floor. "You can't talk to me like that," Annie roared. "Mason loves me."

"Does he?" Apple laughed. "I suggest you start packing your shit before I do it for you."

"Mason!" Annie called my name again. "Wait, what are you doing? You can't do that!"

I wondered if I should go upstairs and intervene. What about poor little Parker? I felt bad for that kid even though he wasn't mine he deserved a good life. I started toward the stairs when a bag landed halfway down the steps. Shit.

"What else do you need to take? Diaper bag for your kid?" Apple asked. "By the way, Annie, who is his real father?"

"Fuck you!" Annie swore.

Apple laughed.

"You're fucking nuts, you know that?" Annie exclaimed.

"I'm nuts?" Apple asked. "Babe, I'm not the one who had to blackmail a man to be with her. Now get the rest of your shit together and get the *fuck* out of this house."

I reminded myself never to get on Apple's bad side as I heard the sound of footsteps over my head. I moved quickly to sit down on the couch and tried to act like everything was normal. I grabbed my phone and pretended to be scrolling through Facebook as the two women came down the stairs.

"You're just going to sit there, Mason, and let her do this? Let her kick your son out? We talked about this." When I slid my eyes up to look at Annie, she had Parker in his car seat with his diaper bag over her shoulder. Apple was holding a small suitcase which I assumed had a few of her other things in it.

"By saying we talked about this, you mean blackmailing me?" I used air quotes to assure her I wasn't playing games anymore.

Annie's nostrils flared as she tried to control herself. "You... how... ugh!" She stomped her feet like a child before she pointed a finger at me. "You're going to regret this." She turned to Apple. "And, you!"

Apple smirked. "Do your worse, sweetie, because whatever it is you think you're going to do to me? I'll do it ten times over," she warned.

"I hate you!" Annie cried before she grabbed the suitcase from Apple's hands. "Just wait until Henry hears about this. You're both going to regret this." She started toward the front door.

Apple's eyes darted to me. "Make sure to tell Henry that I was the one that kicked you out!"

Annie fired off another bunch of expletives which I chose to ignore and then she slammed the door behind her. The locksmith was scheduled to come to the house in less than an hour. After that we would be going to the police station so that I could get a restraining order against Annie. I wouldn't do anything else unless she released any information about London.

As for my plans for London? First, I would win her back. Prove to her that I loved her, that I had always loved her, and that I would never not love her. How I would do that was yet to be figured out, but I knew with Apple's help I could do that.

Hopefully once I made everything right Shepard would forgive me, and Sully, too. Which would make Finn come around. The same with Harper, and I already knew Lake wasn't really pissed at me.

Apple sat down next to me. "Boo, let's figure out our next plan of attack. Get you your girl back." She brushed a piece of blonde hair from her face.

We put our heads together to make a plan. A plan that had to work so I could get my life back, bring my girl home with me, and get my happily ever fucking after.

Chapter Twenty-Two

London

It had been a week since Tessa and I sat down to talk about moving in together. Today we spent the entire day looking at apartments and it didn't go as well as we had hoped it would. We looked at four places. Four shitty, dumpy apartments, and not one of them was what we needed or even close. There had been a fifth one on the list, but we figured after the last one we would just call it a day and try again later.

The first one had only one bedroom after the listing said two, but the second one was so small it could hardly fit a bed inside, making me think it was a closet that they said was a freaking bedroom. The second had two bedrooms, but no washer and dryer hookup. Now, neither one of us had an issue with going to the laundromat, but the closest one was thirty minutes away which didn't seem worth it. The third apartment had the smallest kitchen I had ever seen in my life. Not even enough room for two people to fit inside and the fourth one? Well, let's just say it was six floors with no elevator and that didn't sound like much fun to us.

It was back to the drawing board for us.

"This sucks." Tessa landed face-first on my bed. "How many places are we going to have to look at before we find the right one?"

"You know, Rand said that he was thinking of converting the space over the garage into an apartment and said we could live there if we wanted."

Tessa sat up and flipped over to look at me. "What?" Her eyes were wide. "When did he say that?"

"This morning over breakfast." I tightened my ponytail. "I didn't want to ruin our day together, but wouldn't that be perfect?" I knew that Brooklyn would find some sort of way to keep me close, and honestly, I thought it would be much better for us both.

"Uh, yes!" Tess squealed. She went to hug me, but stopped suddenly. "Did you hear that?"

"No—"

"There it is again!" Tessa's head flew around as she tried to figure out where the sound was coming from. She moved over to the bathroom, but then moved to the closet before she went to the window by my desk. "Uh, Lon, I think you might want to come over here."

I rolled my eyes as I headed over. "It's probably a bird or... holy shit."

Mason was climbing up the side of the house like a prince trying to rescue his princess. Sure, he was using a ladder, but he was still doing it.

I opened the window and stuck my head outside. "What are you doing? You're going to kill yourself out there."

Mason cracked a smile as he looked up to see me watching him. "Saving you, baby." His hand gripped the ladder so tight his knuckles were white.

"Saving me from what, Mason?"

"I should go." Tessa hooked her purse over her shoulder. "Text me and let me know how this goes." She gave me a quick hug. "Bye!" She hurried off as I turned back to find Mason climbing through my window.

"Well," He swung himself up into my room. "Maybe you're going to save me." His hands reached up to cup my face, but I took a step back. "What I did was wrong, London, and I'm sorry."

"Understatement."

He glanced up at the ceiling before his eyes moved back to me. "She blackmailed me, baby. She went to my grandfather and told him that the kid was mine. It wasn't mine. I wore a condom just like I told you, but Henry didn't listen to me. Then Annie said she would go to the press, tell them that you tried to commit suicide. Henry told me if I didn't stay with her he would fire me, he would fire Lake, and—"

"You did this to protect me?" I whispered. My legs suddenly felt like they couldn't hold my own body weight any longer.

Mason nodded.

"But—"

He moved faster than I expected, his arms wrapping around my body to pull me against his muscled chest. "No, no buts," Mason murmured before he slid his lips against mine. "London, I am here to make this right. I will spend the rest of my life and yours trying to make this up to you. I shouldn't have left you at the altar, because marrying you? That would have made me whole."

I clung to Mason like I was afraid he would disappear if I didn't. "You could have just let her go to the press and make a fool of herself. Releasing my personal medical information to the public like that is illegal. She would go to jail, she would lose her kid, and none of this would have happened."

I watched as his brows dipped. "I did it to protect you, baby." His husky voice sent shivers down my spine.

"But, your ride—"

"My ride isn't going anywhere. I spoke to Peter before I came over here this morning. Told him everything that happened, what Henry had threatened to do and he said that my ride was safe. Lake's too. He was going to see about buying out the rest of my grandfather's business from him so that going forward this wouldn't happen again. Not to mention talk to NASCAR about what he did." Mason brushed pieces of stray hair from my face. "Either way? I don't care. You're all I need to make me happy." He put his face against my hair.

Everything that Mason had done, he had done for me. To protect me because he loved me, and to protect Lake because, well, he loved him, too, in some way or another. Yes, I was angry. I was angry that Annie would do something like this because she was crazy enough to try to get Mason to be with her, but I wasn't angry with him. How could I be?

Mason pulled back to look at me. "Hey." He let his fingers dance over my temple. "What's going on inside that mind, baby? Talk to me." He tried to step back, but I wouldn't let him.

"I was thinking about how selfless you were doing all of this."

"That so?"

I smiled up at him. "I missed you." My voice caught in my throat and for a second I thought I was going to cry, but I was able to hold the tears back.

"Oh, baby, not as much as I missed you." Mason's mouth found mine again, but this time he nibbled hungrily on my bottom lip, telling me that he needed more than just a kiss if this continued. "I need you." He groaned softly. "All of you, London. Right now, right here before I lose my mind." He cupped my ass with his big hands.

I watched Mason under my lashes as he let me take a step back and began to remove my clothes. I pulled my shirt up over my head first and then shrugged off my jeans. As I started to slide the straps of my bra down over my shoulders, it was hard not to notice the bulge that was pressing against Mason's pants.

"You like that, don't you?" He growled as he gripped his dick with his hand. "How hard you make me?"

I nodded. "Yes," I cooed as I reached back to unhook my bra and then that, too, landed on the floor leaving me in nothing but my underwear.

"Fuck, you are so gorgeous, baby. I can't wait to be inside you again. I almost forgot what that little pussy feels like." Mason was already tugging off his jeans so that he could climb up onto the bed. He patted the mattress and I joined him. "Lie down," he instructed and when I did he pressed his hard, thick body against mine.

"I love you." The words tumbled from my mouth and I watched as a smile slipped up Mason's face.

"I know, baby, and I love you." He slid his lips across mine before he moved his mouth down my neck. "I love everything about you." Mason kissed my skin. "Your beautiful tits." He licked at my right nipple and I cried out as pleasure ran through my body. I arched my back as his tongue rolled around the taut skin. "Both actually." He chuckled as he ran his tongue across my chest to get to the left one next and repeated the same assault.

"Mason." I dug my nails into his back. "Stop torturing me." The way he made me feel was like nothing I had ever felt before.

Mason's lips fluttered against my skin as he moved down my stomach. "Relax, baby, and let me make you feel good. Don't rush it." His tongue tickled my belly button just as his fingers began to pull down my underwear. "Are you ready?" Mason looked up at me with hooded eyes.

Before I could answer Mason had already ripped my panties from my body, another pair ruined by my man, and he dragged his tongue between my slick folds. My hips bucked up as I tried not to scream out his name. Instead, I gripped his hair and tried to keep Mason where I needed him. Where I wanted him.

Mason pushed my thighs apart. "It's not like you're not going to come more than once." I could feel him smirk against me as his tongue tantalized and teased me. Before long I was lost in the licking, petting, and lashing as I gripped Mason's hair tightly as I tried not to give in to the wave that threatened to push me over the edge.

Mason climbed up over my body. "You're holding back on me, baby." He ran a finger across my lips before he leaned down to kiss me. I grabbed the back of his neck to keep his head in place and he growled as my tongue found his. Mason's heavy cock was pressed against me as our tongues tangled together and I couldn't help but try to urge him inside. He began to ease himself inside me inch by painfully slow inch.

My pussy stretched for Mason like it always did and I moaned softly as he filled me so fucking good. I arched my hips to meet his, as we began to move together, still locked together in a kiss neither one of us wanted to end. Mason's arms wrapped around my back as he pulled me closer and he rubbed against my insides in a way no one *ever* fucking could. I was so dizzy with desire that I wasn't sure how much longer I would be able to hold back.

"Fuck, London." Mason's voice was thick with desire. He began to jerk himself faster inside me. "So good, baby. So wet and perfect." His lips danced against mine as his dick pushed me closer to the release I desperately wanted. "Come with me, baby," he demanded and I did.

I cried out as the orgasm threatened to rip me in two. I clamped my eyes shut at the same time as I did the same around Mason's shaft, and I might have screamed his name if his mouth still wasn't covering mine. His own release thrilled me as he grunted and groaned as he sprayed my insides until I was sure it would just spill out onto the sheets. Mason stayed there for a moment as he tried to catch his breath before he slipped onto the bed and wrapped his strong arms around me.

"You're coming home with me tonight."

I smiled. "Home?"

Mason opened one eye. "Yes, baby, home. The house I bought for *us*. It won't be home until you're there with me." He slid his mouth across mine. "Then we'll get married the proper way. With friends, family, fuck a clown and farm animals, too, if you want." His eyes sparkled happily.

"I only want you there," I assured him as I moved to climb off the bed. His hand reached out to stop me and he pulled me back. "Mason—"

"Tell me that you're going to come with me, London." His voice sounded full of worry. "I don't want to be there without you, and if you won't go there? I'm going to stay here."

I tilted my head before I reached over to cup his scruffy jaw in my hand. "Of course, Mason," I assured him. I cuddled against him so that I could rest my head against his chest.

"Rand told me his brother is back."

"He didn't take it very well." I ran my fingers over the hard muscles of his abdomen. "I'm not sure of their backstory, but maybe they can work it out."

Mason grabbed my hand. "I wouldn't count on that," he told me. "I'd stop that if I were you, baby, because if you don't—"

"If I don't, what?" I teased with heat in my voice. I slithered up over him so that I could straddle his waist. I felt moisture bead between my legs when Mason's hand wrapped gently around my throat.

"You might get fucked again." He smirked. "Or is that what you want?"

Raw need flashed in Mason's eyes as I nodded.

"Giddy up, cowgirl." He grinned.

It would be awhile before we finally left that room, and when we did, I wouldn't go back there again.

Chapter Twenty-Three

MASON

Before I went to get London from Rand's place I had actually spoken to him and Sully. I didn't want to just show up there without them knowing what I was doing and what I had planned. I was kind of scared Shepard might try to beat the shit out of me, if I'm being honest. The three of us actually sat down and talked like civil humans while London was out with Tessa looking at apartments.

That's also how I knew about Eli being back.

Sully wasn't pissed at me. She was pissed at Annie. Girl was a pretty cool chick now that I had gotten to know her. After all the years I thought she hated me, honestly she had every right to, she was now one of my biggest supporters. She said that I should have Annie thrown in jail for what she did, but I was more worried about Parker. I just wanted her to stay away from me and so all I did was file a restraining order against her.

"You don't know who Parker's dad is?" Rand asked as he ran his hands through his hair. He looked super stressed out. I couldn't blame him. He had his brother to worry about, and another baby on the way.

I shook my head. "Nope, no clue. Annie wouldn't tell me because she insisted I was the dad." I told them both how I wore a condom, and that I never even came inside said condom. "Too bad because he's a cute shit." I nodded at Brooklyn. "When are you due?"

She pressed both hands to her swollen stomach. "Any day

now, and honestly, I can't wait. I'm so fat, so swollen, and ready to have her." Her face turned red. "I can't hide it anymore, Rand."

"Darlin', it's fine. People will know soon enough anyway." He touched her face. "You should go lie down. You look exhausted." Rand helped her to her feet. "Don't go anywhere, we need to talk." He glanced over at me for a second. "I'll be right back."

"Good luck, Mason." Sully patted my shoulder before she leaned down and kissed my cheek.

I sat there for a second as I waited for Rand to come back and looked around the kitchen. The fridge was covered in crayon drawings that RJ had done. I got up to get a closer look and I assumed they were of his father's car.

"Cute, right?" Rand's voice made me jump. He grinned proudly at me when I turned to face him. "You and London ever talk about kids? I mean, I know that she can't have children, but you could adopt." He sat back down at the table, so I followed.

"No."

"I get it. Like Brooklyn and me, right? It just sort of happened. You love her so much it fucking hurts. She's all you can think about, all you dream about?" Rand put his hands on the table. "So, what do you think I should do about my brother?"

I knew Eli from when I used to hang out with him, Lake, and Cooper. Before Rand was racing in NASCAR. "I'm not sure, man. That's your call, but obviously he wants to make things right between the two of you."

Rand was on his feet again. "Said he was clean, Brian gave him a job." He stopped to look at me. "I swear to fucking God if he's driving I will lose my shit." He shook his head. "Brian wouldn't do that to me."

Brian Porter was Rand and Finn's car owner. "I don't think he'd do that either, bro. Eli's been gone for how long now?" Shit, he wouldn't do that, would he? That would be seriously fucked-up.

Rand stopped pacing. "Seven years or so. Last time I heard from him was right after my first race. I knew he was hammered because I could hear it in his voice, but he sounded so proud of me." He slammed his fist against the countertop so hard the bowl of fruit shook. "Fuck." He gritted his teeth.

"What did he want when he came here?" I asked.

"I think maybe he thought I was going to welcome him back with open fucking arms. He had the nerve to try to talk to me about my wife." Rand finally sat back down. "I told him to fuck off. God, he has some balls."

My brows shot up. "Gee, sounds familiar." I snickered when his eyes shot over to me. "Maybe you should talk to him."

"Maybe you should fuck off."

Okay.

"Eli royally screwed me over, man, and it's going to take a lot more than him coming here to tell me he's clean to get me to just forgive him or talk to him." Rand drummed his fingers against the table. "I'm sure he'll come begging to all his buddies, too."

"I'm not his buddy anymore," I reminded him. Eli fucked me over, too. Stole some cash, some clothes, and a car from me. Not that I ever reported that, but it still hurt when I thought we were friends.

Rand's eyes met mine. "Good." He nodded and leaned back in the chair. "Now, what are you going to do about London?"

Once I got London home to our house we didn't leave for three days, and that was only because I had a race to go to. We spent pretty much the entire time christening every room in every single way we could imagine and finally ended up in the soaking tub, which was something I had been dying to try with her.

"I can't believe you bought a house." London leaned her head against my chest as we sat in the warm water the night before I had to leave.

I scooped water up into my hand so that I could dribble it down her chest just to hear London's laugh. "I'll buy you the world, baby," I whispered into her ear. She was tucked between my legs perfectly. Like she was made for me.

London sighed happily. "I don't want the world, Mason." She tilted her head so that we had to look at one another. "I just want you."

"No worries there."

London adjusted herself so that she was now facing me in the tub. "And, a baby," she confessed before she looked down at the soapy water. "I know that... I can't carry your child, but maybe we could find someone else that could." When she looked up at me again her blues shined with hope.

I moved across the tub so fast that water spilled over the sides, but I didn't care. "Baby." I brushed my lips across hers. "If you want a child? We'll have a child. We'll adopt or we'll do the surrogate thing. Whatever it takes," I assured her as London's arms came up around my neck. "Come with me this weekend," I suggested.

London hesitated. "I don't know if that's such a great idea." She chewed on her bottom lip.

I knew how she always associated the track with Cooper, but I could help her change that. Make her think of us and *only* us. My hands skimmed down her torso and I felt London shiver. "Think of how much fun we could have," I murmured as I ran my nose against her neck. "I can show you off to everyone so they can see my sexy fucking girlfriend." I dragged my teeth over her skin which caused her to whimper.

London's eyes fluttered as my hands brushed over her chest, down her stomach and between her legs. She opened her thighs eagerly while she licked her lips as I let my fingers spread her open and then I paused for a brief moment. Her eyes were closed, her mouth opened slightly, and she had her hands against her tits which made my dick throb.

"What... Mason!" She blushed when she caught me watching.

"You are so fucking beautiful," I reminded her. Someday, someday London would realize just how gorgeous she was. Not just to me, but to every man that saw her.

"Yes," she whispered softly as I went to kiss her. "I'll go with you." She gave me a bright smile when our eyes met.

"Really?" I didn't want to get my hopes up, but I just knew having London there would be a good luck charm.

She nodded.

I jumped out of the tub with excitement. "Awesome!" I grabbed a towel for her as she joined me. "This is going to be so much fun. Wait." I just had a thought about Brooklyn being pregnant. "What about your sister?"

"I can fly home if something happens. Just like Rand," London reminded me as she wrapped the towel around her thin frame.

"Right, right." I hugged her against me. "This is going to be so awesome, baby, you'll see." I assured her.

London flashed me a big smile as she dried off her hair with a smaller towel. "I know it is. I'm actually looking forward to it. I've never been to Michigan before." She giggled softly.

I grabbed London and spun her around before I picked her up off her feet. "I love you. Fuck, you're amazing." I placed her back on her feet. "Thank you."

Friday morning London and I arrived in Michigan. I was the happiest I had been in months coming to a race, and as we made our way to my RV, I dropped her hand to wrap my arm around her waist.

"The last time you came to a race was when, baby?" I nodded at a couple of drivers as we walked.

London leaned into me. "I've only been to one," she confessed.

"Really?" I noticed a couple of guys giving me strange looks as we walked. What? Like I wasn't allowed to bring a girl with me. Okay, well the only woman I had ever brought to a race with me had been Apple, but we weren't a couple so I had never been this close with her.

"Yep."

I noticed my RV up ahead, so I pulled my key from my pocket to unlock the door. "Then this will be the best one for you," I assured her. I would make sure of that.

"Mason." London's voice was tight. "Why is everyone watching us?" Her eyes looked almost scared when we stepped inside. Then she looked around to see all the roses I had made sure were placed inside before we got there. "What... Mason, what is this?" she whispered.

I got down on one knee. "Marry me," I asked as I produced the ring from my other pocket. The one that didn't have my keys in it. "I know you're not big on people watching or staring so I made sure to do it here, in private so no one could see, but I love you so fucking much," I told her.

London was staring down at the ring in the box. I didn't want to go crazy with the ring, although I wanted to get the biggest fucking diamond on the face of the planet for my woman. According to Sully, London didn't even like diamonds, so I'm glad I asked before I went and bought the ring. The ring I had picked out was black gold with a one carat emerald in the middle. It was the most beautiful ring I had ever seen and perfect for my future wife.

"London?" I stared up at her.

"That is the most amazing ring I have ever seen." She held out her hand and I noticed how it shook. "Yes, Mason." Tears slipped down her cheeks. "I'll marry you." She nodded her head. The ring looked perfect on her finger, but I knew that it would.

"Kiss me." I got up so that I could brush my mouth against London's, but she grabbed my shirt to keep it going. Her tongue easing between my lips until I growled and couldn't think about anything other than burying myself inside her. I might have if someone didn't rudely knock at the door.

I ripped the door open. "What?" I demanded, only to find Finn standing there. "Er, sorry. What's up?" I tried to brush off my rudeness.

Finn shoved his phone up to the door. "This is what's up." He glared at me.

I didn't use my twitter often or any social media, but I had it because I needed it from time to time. Apparently I was trending though, and not in a good way. "What's going on? Why am I—?"

"That bitch!" London exclaimed and I spun around. "She fucking did it."

"She... oh shit."

London showed me her phone this time.

Mason Pelletier's girlfriend attempts suicide after he tries to break up with her. Hospital papers to prove it.

I felt my blood begin to fucking boil. "That bitch." I was going to have her put in jail so fast her head would spin. But there was more.

Rand Sullivan's sister-in-law has a long history of depression and an eating disorder after being sexually assaulted by late driver, Cooper Houston.

How could Annie do something like this? How could she hate me or London so much? How could she be so evil?

"Mason, I don't... I can't... I have to leave." London was already heading toward the door where Finn was still standing, but I was quicker than she was.

"Baby, you can't. We have to—"

"What?" We have to what, exactly? You fucking told me she wouldn't do this! Everything is out there now! This is my life, and you ruined it! My biggest, darkest secret is out there for the entire world to see."

I shook with rage at what Annie had done. "I didn't do this, baby, you know I didn't," I tried to assure her, but I could see London's mind was already made up. "Please don't leave. I need you." I couldn't bear the thought of being without her again.

London's phone started to ring. "It's Sully." She turned away from me to answer it.

"We're suing her." Rand appeared behind Finn. "I don't care what we have to do, but that bitch is going to jail for the rest of her life."

"I'm leaving." London hit end on the phone. "I'm... I can't stay here, Mason." Her brows dipped down. "I'm not leaving you, just here." She flashed a quick smile, but the tears that filled her eyes did little to hide my doubts and fears.

"I love you," I whispered.

"I know."

I stood there as I watched London step out of the RV that just minutes before had been my happy place. She ducked her head down to hide her face and walked away without even looking back. Rand and Finn both followed her while I stood there doing nothing.

Then I picked up my phone to call my lawyer. I was going to fucking fix this if it was the last thing I did.

Chapter Twenty-Four

I was sick to my stomach at what Annie had done. I was a fighter, I would bounce back and get over this, but how dare she do this to Mason? He tried to protect me from that witch by moving her into his, no, *our* house with a kid that wasn't even his *for me*. Mason didn't do any of that to save himself or because Annie wanted him to, but because he didn't want my personal information getting out.

I'd be lying if I wasn't upset about the Cooper thing getting out. That was a secret I never intended to share with anyone until Mason came along. Until he did the right thing and told Sully, but how did Annie know? Did she listen in on our conversation?

Finn and Rand had both made sure I got on a plane, safely, to go back to North Carolina. I should have gone back to our place, but instead I was currently in an Uber headed to Sully's. I needed my sister even though I had texted both Tess and Rush. I was worried about Rush since I hadn't heard from him much these days, but I only hoped that meant he was just busy.

"I'm so sorry." Brooklyn rushed out to wrap her arms around me when I climbed up the steps to her house. "That bitch, Lon, I've already talked to Mason." She soothed the hair around my head.

I blinked. "What?"

"He contacted his lawyer. What Annie did could get her fined a lot of money, and some possible jail time. It's a HIPAA violation to release your personal medical information. She was your nurse and she worked at the hospital you were at. She might lose her nursing license, too." Sully's brows dipped. "Did you not talk to Mason? London, did you just run instead of talking this over with him? Shit." The dark circles under her eyes worried me.

I shook my head. "I didn't... well okay, but I told him I just needed to get out of there. I didn't want to bring more unwanted attention to myself. Do you want to go inside and sit down?" I asked as my sister closed her eyes.

Brooklyn nodded, so I followed her inside the house. "RJ's on a playdate with Frankie, Noah, Noel, and Kayla." She advised as she dropped onto the couch. I watched as she struggled to lift her swollen ankles up onto the coffee table.

"Kayla?"

"Harper insisted she tag along. I think that she just wanted to get out of the house."

I chuckled. "Sounds like Harper." I sat back against the chair. "So, Mason called his lawyer?" We needed to get back on track with this clusterfuck.

"Right after you left." Sully grimaced. "Fucking Christ, I am so ready to not be pregnant anymore." She grumbled and shifted on the couch.

"Are you alright?" I stood up as I saw the pained look on my sister's face.

"I'm pretty sure my water just broke."

"Wait, what?"

Brooklyn waved her hand at me. "Relax, London. I've done

this before. Go get my phone off the charger in the kitchen. I need to call the doctor, Rand, and Harper. Then I'm going to need you to drive me to the hospital." She grinned at me like she did this every single day.

I rushed into the kitchen to do as she asked, thankful that I was here when Brooklyn needed me. Happy to be able to help and be reliable for the first time in a very long time before I hurried back to hand her the cell phone.

My sister was giving birth. I was about to be an aunt again and for a little while everything else was forgotten.

———

Sage Joy Shepard was born fourteen hours later. She weighed seven pounds exactly and was twenty inches long. She was the most beautiful baby I had ever seen in my life with the porcelain skin of a baby doll, thick dark hair and purplish-blue eyes.

Rand made it just in time for the delivery, and to say he was a proud father might be the understatement of the century. He hadn't left Sully's side since the baby was born and didn't want to put Sage down for anyone. I knew the moment he saw his daughter no man or woman would ever be good enough for her, and I felt bad for whoever she brought home for the first time.

"Mr. Shepard," the nurse exclaimed. "You can't expect to hold your daughter the entire time," she scolded.

"Watch me."

I hid my smile as I turned to see Harper walk in as the nurse strolled out in a huff. She shifted Kayla's car seat from one hand to another. "I think someone wants to meet his baby sister." She gave RJ a little nudge as he peeked around her legs.

Brooklyn patted the bed. "Come sit with me, baby," she said groggily. Pushing a watermelon out of your vagina sure made you tired, I thought, and a pang of guilt hit me. I hadn't even texted Mason, and he probably thought I fucking hated him.

As RJ climbed up into the bed I ducked out of the room and down the hall to get a little privacy. Rand had someone drive for him today, but Mason would still be at the track. I punched his name into the phone as I slipped outside, but after a few rings, it went to voicemail.

"You've reached Mason—"

I hung up. He probably had meetings and interviews before the race. He was busy being important and I was just me. My phone buzzed in my hand as I stared up at the blue sky and I was surprised to see it was from Mason.

Mason: *How's the baby? I'm in the driver's meeting or I would have answered.*

I smiled as I attached a picture of Sage and hit send.

Mason: *She's beautiful. Shepard must be over the moon.*

I dragged my teeth over my lip as I thought about what I should say next.

Mason: *I miss you.*

Shit, he was trying to kill me.

Mason: *Are you still there?*

I finally answered back.

London: *Yes, sorry, just trying to figure out what to say. I feel stupid for leaving. I should have stayed to support you. To show that we were a unit and no matter what she did, we weren't going anywhere.*

When Mason didn't respond I figured he got busted for using his phone which was a huge no-no in those meetings, but instead my own rang in my hand as I prepared to slip it into my back pocket.

"You're not stupid, baby." Mason's voice was husky as he spoke. "You had every single right to be upset with what happened. Annie's already been arrested," he told me.

"What?"

"This morning according to Don, my lawyer, and she's being held on a million-dollar bond that she won't be able to post." Mason sighed. "Parker has been taken into foster care until something else can be arranged. I'm not sure she has any family around here or if she'll admit to who his real father is."

I knew, even if he didn't want to admit it, Mason obviously cared for Parker. Suddenly, an idea popped into my head. "Mason." I swallowed. "What about us?"

"What about us... oh." He didn't speak for a minute and I thought maybe we got disconnected. "Baby, are you sure because I don't want Parker to be a constant reminder of Annie hanging over you. Hanging over us."

God, what did I do to deserve this man? "He's innocent in all of this," I reminded him. "Just a baby who was born to a wicked bitch of a mother." I wanted to say much worse, but changed my mind.

"London, hold on one second," Mason told me, followed by the muffled sound of talking. "I'm sorry, baby, but I gotta go before they fine me for missing any more of the meeting." Not a lie there. "Look, I'll get in touch with Don again about Parker before the race starts."

"Good luck today." I smiled into the phone. "I should have stayed."

"You're with Sully which is exactly where you need to be right now," Mason reminded me. "I love you. I'll call you later." He hung up before I had the chance to tell him I loved him, too, so I made sure I texted him and then went back inside.

"You good?" Rand asked as I stepped back into the room. He was still holding his daughter while it looked like Brooklyn had finally fallen asleep. He might never let Sage go at this rate and she'd be going to senior prom with her father. The thought made me giggle.

"I'm great," I assured him. "We're did Harper go?" RJ was missing, too.

"Down to the gift shop where I'm sure RJ will come back with a balloon for himself, his sister, and everyone else." He tilted his head. "Are you really doing great or are you just saying that because you know it's what I want to hear?"

I stepped closer. "I'm really fucking great, Shepard." I spun the ring on my finger and realized I never even told Sully Mason proposed to me with everything that had happened.

"Nice, right?" He jutted his chin at my hand. "Show me."

"My ring?"

"No, you're fucking tramp stamp, yes your ring." Rand rolled his eyes. His lips turned up into a big smile when I did as he asked. "Fucking good job, Pelletier," he muttered.

My heart swelled against my ribs. "For your information." I smirked. "I don't have a tramp stamp." I stuck my tongue out when Rand chuckled. "Can I hold Sage?" I hadn't actually had the chance, not with mister hoggy pants, and probably for the first time in my life I actually *wanted* to hold a baby.

"Of course."

My breath caught in my lungs as I sat down so Rand could place my niece into my arms. She was so tiny, so perfect, and so amazing. Wrapped in a rosy pink blanket with a hat on her head that matched. Her eyelids fluttered as she slept, which made me wonder what she might be dreaming about.

"Pretty cool, right?" Rand's eyes were on his daughter as he spoke. "I missed out on so much with RJ, but that was my own damn fault. This time? This time I'm not going to miss a thing." He reached down to run his finger lightly across Sage's forehead.

We sat like that for a few minutes in silence, but our quiet moment ended the moment RJ came bursting into the room complete with balloons. Rand winked at me when he grabbed his son and hugged him tightly.

"What do you say you and I go get something to eat, buddy?" He hooked him against his hip. "Let the girls talk for a bit?"

"Can I bring my balloon?" RJ tugged on the race car balloon tied around his wrist.

"Absolutely," Rand assured him. "We'll be back." He gave a little wave before he took RJ and headed out of the room. RJ wrapped his arms around his father's neck as they went down the hall, and I realized how badly I wanted to give that to Mason. He deserved that, too.

Chapter Twenty-Five

London

"He let you hold the baby?" Sully's sleepy voice brought my attention over to where she was watching me. She adjusted herself up higher on the pillows. "Well, wonders never do cease." She grinned at me.

Harper sat down next to me before she placed the car seat on the floor. Kayla was watching her with big eyes. "Are you excited to meet your new best friend?" She tickled her daughter, who giggled happily. "Come here, sweetie." Harper unbuckled her to bring her up onto her lap.

We all watched as Kayla's gray eyes zoomed right in on Sage who was still sleeping peacefully in my arms. She looked at her mother, back at the baby, her mother again, and then pointed to the baby. "Baabaa?"

Harper nodded. "Yes, Kay, baby." She hugged her daughter close.

I smiled as I glanced at my sister. "Should we go?" I could see the exhaustion written all over her face.

"Not until you show me your engagement ring."

"What?" Harper exclaimed, but she clamped a hand over her mouth when Sage's eyes flew open. The baby stared at her for a second before she went right back to sleep like nothing had even happened. "Mason proposed?" She dropped her hand so that she could hiss at me between clenched teeth.

I blushed. "Yes." I couldn't exactly hold up my hand so Harper leaned down to check it out.

"Shit, that's beautiful." She nodded her approval.

I managed to get to my feet so that I could walk over to Brooklyn, who took her daughter from me. Then I showed her the ring. "You helped him, didn't you?" I asked as she turned my hand to get a better look.

Sully shrugged her shoulders as she let me take my hand back. "I might have." She adjusted Sage against her chest as she sat back. "He asked for my help, so I gave it to him. All I've ever wanted was for you to be happy. I believe that you'll find that with Mason."

"Me, too." I squeezed Brooklyn's wrist. "I'm glad that I'm here. That I was able to be here for the birth of the baby, but I wish I was with Mason, too. Can we turn on the race?" I asked. That would at least help a little bit.

Harper coughed. "My man is racing, too, you know." She grinned at me when I rolled my eyes.

We turned on the television and flipped through the stations to find the race before Harper and I both moved our chairs around Sully's bed so we could all watch together. When Rand walked back into the room, he found the three of us laughing, giggling and having fun. He leaned against the doorframe with his arm crossed as RJ climbed up onto the bed.

"Mia's on her way up with the boys," he told us. "Ran into her in the gift shop. Just thought I'd give you all a heads-up." He maneuvered his way around the chairs before he sat down on the bed next to his wife, newborn daughter, and son. "How are you feeling, darlin'?" He slid his lips across Brooklyn's forehead as he gazed down at her.

I let my eyes move around the room and felt happiness swell inside me. For the first time in my entire life I finally felt like my life was actually normal. I was just missing my fiancé, who, I would have back in my arms as soon as this race was over.

Then everything would be complete.

I left the hospital right after the race ended, exhausted, but happy to have spent the day with my family and friends. I don't remember the last time I had enjoyed myself that much. Let myself relax, laugh, and not worry about what others might be thinking about me. My therapist would be so proud when I told her.

The Uber dropped me off at Mason's place, wait, *our* place, and I hurried inside so that I could shower before he got home. I was halfway up the walkway when I noticed someone sitting on the front porch.

Who in the fuck?

"You must be London." He stood up as I got closer, and I wished that I could get to my phone without him noticing.

I narrowed my eyes as I took him in. Tall, nearly six feet, with gray hair, and brown eyes, that were anything but friendly as they watched me. His face, which was probably handsome when he was younger, was lined with wrinkles, while his lips were pressed into a thin, tight line.

"You're Henry," I burst out before I could stop myself.

"Mason's grandfather, this...everything that has happened to us is because of you." My chest felt tight as I continued to stare at him.

Henry's lips turned up into a smile that didn't meet his eyes. "He's spoken about me?" He tilted his head up.

"No." I shook my head. "Don't do that, Mr. Pelletier, he only told me what you did to him. What you did to us, and how you let that woman—"

"Sweetheart, I think you're getting ahead of yourself. Annie and I..." He stopped to move down the steps, but didn't attempt to come closer to me. "She wasn't supposed to release that information. She let her jealousy get the better of her, even with the child we created, and now? Well, now I'm here to try to fix that."

Henry is Parker's father? If that's the truth that would make him Mason's uncle. I felt sick to my stomach.

Henry's eyes flicked over me. "I can see that your little brain is working which only means you've figured it out without me having to tell you. You know, London," He took a step toward me which made me take one back. "I can see why my grandson would want to pick you over Annie. You're younger, you're prettier, and obviously a lot smarter. I just don't understand why he would want to settle *down* with you."

I squared my shoulders as I tried to figure a way out of this. "You should leave." My voice sounded a lot stronger than I felt.

Henry took another step. "I guess it's the whole abused little girl thing that probably got him. If Cooper Houston hadn't dirtied you up like he did, Mason probably wouldn't have looked in your direction." Another step. "You're not his usual type."

I took two steps back only to collide with something thick, solid, and... "Mason," I whispered his name as I felt his chest at my back. One of his arms wrapped around my waist protectively as his grandfather locked eyes with him.

"Apologize."

"Son—"

Mason's hand tightened around me. "I fucking said, apologize to my fiancée." He growled from deep in his chest. "You have some fucking nerve coming here, to our home, old man. Talking to my woman like that..." His voice trailed off and I could feel the heat boiling from his body.

Henry blinked slowly at his grandson. "You're confused, son, you don't know what you're saying. Pussy can do that—"

Mason's arm was suddenly gone from my body as he lunged for his grandfather. He gripped Henry's shirt collar between his fists as he stared down at him. "Stop calling me, son, Henry, because we both know that I was never your fucking son," he seethed. "You don't get to talk to London like that. Do you understand me?" He glanced at me for a second before he looked back at the man in front of him. "No, scratch that. You don't get to talk to London, you don't get to look at her. You fucking apologize and you leave before I call the police to have you removed from my property. Don't you dare come back. Ever." Mason loosened his grip.

Henry smoothed his shirt down. "You're going to regret this," he snapped. "You'll have no job, no car, *nothing* to keep her here."

Mason's hand shot out and he hit his grandfather square in the jaw. The impact sent him backward, but he caught himself before he fell. "Get the fuck out before I hit you again," he warned.

Henry didn't say another word as he began to walk and Mason moved so that he could wrap his arm around my shoulders.

"You're okay? He didn't touch you or do anything?" He used the knuckles of his right hand to turn my face to look up at him.

"I'm fine, Mason," I assured him. "Parker's your uncle." I waited for his reaction.

"I know." He stopped me before I could speak again. "I found out before I got here, baby, after talking to Don. Seems Annie is trying everything she possibly can to get herself out of prison and that was the little bomb she dropped this morning." Mason's lips turned up into a smile. "Let's go inside our house so we can talk more in private." He scooped me up before I had a chance to fight him and carried me up the steps. He placed me on my feet so that he could unlock the front door, and the moment the door was shut, he caged me in against the front door with eyes hooded with want.

We never even made it to the bedroom.

———

"That's how much I missed you." Mason ran his nose against my neck as we cuddled on the living room couch.

I giggled as I moved closer. I still had on my right sock, but the left one was somewhere in the living room. Mason had torn my underwear off before throwing them onto the coffee table, my bra was hanging off of the lamp, my jeans were in the front hallway, and my shirt? My shirt was either on the floor or maybe we were lying on it. Mason had managed to drop all of his clothes in a pile by the couch before he pounced on me, but I wasn't keeping score or anything.

"Is that so?" I asked as I breathed in his scent. Gasoline, exhaust, and the citrusy smell of his aftershave. Fucking heaven.

Mason shifted his body. "Tomorrow we're going to bring Parker home." He met my eyes with worry. "If it's too fast, let me know, but the sooner he's home, with us, the better. He deserves to be with his family."

My heart jumped in my chest. "Of course, Mason, I want him to be here." A baby? In our house? We were going to be fucking parents, and I couldn't imagine doing that with anyone else.

"You're sure? Because—"

"Mason." I searched his face. "Are you nervous about raising a child?"

He nodded.

I slid my mouth across his. "You're going to be great at it." I climbed up so that I was straddling Mason's waist. "At being a father, I mean. You're so fucking amazing. You've saved me in so many ways I had no idea I needed to be saved. We're going to have all this help from our family and friends. Parker will grow up with so many friends. Sage, Kayla, Frankie, RJ... the twins." I placed both hands against his chest. "We can do this."

"We can do this." He repeated my words as his chestnut eyes danced with happiness.

"You and me. Raising your uncle."

Mason scrunched up his nose. "When you say it like that, it sounds so...so..."

"So *Game of Thrones*-like?" I teased before he flipped me over onto my back.

Mason's hands roamed over my body. Down my ribs, over my hips and finally he tangled them into my hair. "That's exactly what it sounds like, baby," he murmured before he kissed me. I could feel him pressed against my leg, heavy, hard, and ready again. "I fucking love you, London." He nipped at my bottom lip.

I arched my back as heat spread through my core. "I love you, Mason." I moaned as he wrapped my hair around his hand.

"Always."

Epilogue

MASON

Once Parker came home with us, London and I both decided that we would keep his real parents a secret until he was old enough to understand. The only people we did tell were our close friends and family which was hard enough to explain. They understood once we did, but having to do that with the media would be a full-on shit show I wasn't ready to deal with right now.

London took to motherhood better than I ever dreamed she would. We fixed up a room just for Parker, and often at night I would find her in there singing to him songs she had written. Songs that made my heart nearly explode from my chest they were so brilliant and sweet. London never once complained about having to get up in the middle of the night for feedings or diaper changes. She simply did it because she loved Parker, loved having him in our home, and wanted to make him happy.

We've talked about getting married, but haven't set a date yet. I think with everything that has happened and how we fought so hard to get back together, we're just trying to take every day as it comes. Of course, I want to marry London and claim her as my wife. The day that happens will be one of the happiest days of my life. Right up there with the day she told me she was pregnant.

That's right, London is pregnant. She's having my baby and I want to shout it from the rooftops, but right now we're keeping that little secret between the two of us. Because of everything she's been through, she's considered high risk, so we're holding off on the news until we're ready. But, watching her blossom, glow, and grow with this baby has made me realize that I wouldn't want to be a father or a husband or anything else without that woman in my life.

Annie took a plea bargain once she realized Henry gave up who Parker's real father was. I never found out the exact details between her and Henry, but I don't really care to know either. She not only lost her nursing license, but gave up her rights to her only child without even asking how he was. She also isn't allowed within three hundred feet of the three of us or it's back to jail for her.

I know that I once told London that we were bad for one another, but I know now that I was wrong.

We were made for one another because we sure as hell weren't made for anyone else.

London

Two years later

As I pulled my car onto the off-ramp to head toward our house, all I could think about was how Mason was there waiting for me. Probably with celebratory champagne, roses, and chocolate because it was kind of a big day for me right now. I was returning from a trip from Nashville and I had sold not one, but four of my songs. My words were going to be put on a new album by Blake Shelton. Someone needed to pinch me because I honestly felt like this wasn't real life right now. How could all of my dreams be coming true after I'd thought I wasn't worthy of any of them? Or worthy of having dreams of any kind?

I thought I had no purpose in my life until I met Mason. He showed me that I was more than my eating disorder. More than just a number on a scale. I love being a mother and being pregnant was one of the most amazing things to happen in my life and I'm so glad I was able to experience the miracle of childbirth. With the help of Mason, my therapist, my doctor, and my family, I was able to have a healthy, successful pregnancy.

If it wasn't for my husband, I'm not sure I would be where I am today.

That's right; Mason and I finally tied the knot a couple of months before our daughter, Samantha, was born. We had a small wedding that was planned and put together by Sully because I was on bedrest at that point, but with the approval of my doctor, I did get to walk down the aisle. It wasn't anything big or fancy just something we wanted to do with our friends and family before Sam was born. I couldn't fit into Brooklyn's dress this time around, but Mia let me borrow the dress she wore when she got married to her late husband.

We named Sam after Mason's late mother, who I wish I could have met. I know that she would be so proud of the man that her son has become. He won the NASCAR championship this past season and I couldn't go to the award banquet because I was pregnant and the whole bedrest thing. He brought our son, Parker, as his guest, and it was the cutest thing I had ever seen in my life. I know Mason is hoping that Parker will grow up wanting to drive, too, since our friends' kids just started go-kart racing. I keep teasing him that maybe Sami will end up being the racer in the family, but I know in the end Mason won't care if Parker and Sam both decide they don't want anything to do with NASCAR at all.

He's pretty fantastic like that. A great husband, an even better father, and a pretty good friend, too.

My knight. My prince. My savior. My world.

THE END

Acknowledgments

My more than amazing husband — my biggest supporter and for all those nights grilling dinner so that I could get this book done. You have been my rock, my best friend, and everything else that I have needed as I try to get my writing career moving. I know that I couldn't do this without you, baby, and I wouldn't want to. Thank you for being my constant support in this crazy world, and putting up with me. ***Real Love Is Forever.***

Ellen, Sissy, and Dea — I couldn't have asked for better sisters in my life. Thank you for sharing, liking, and even reading the first book even though it might have been a little more graphic than you were used to. Just a warning that this one is a little darker, but I hope you still love me as much as I love you!

Kimmy, Jessica, and Bridget — For the reviews, the support, and being the first three to give feedback. The excitement you've shown makes me hope that this is something I can continue to keep doing.

Kathryn Hansen — In 2013 I was struggling with my own eating disorder and was desperate for a way out. I was binge eating nearly every single weekend, and sometimes during the week. I stumbled across the book Brain Over Binge by Kathryn Hansen on April 1st of that year and I have been binge free ever since. I know that that book saved my life.

Stephanie — it doesn't matter that you live 1500 miles away or that we don't see one another every single day like some best friends. You're my person.

Everyone at AFF — the message board may not be around anymore, but I still remember all the fun we had, the stories we wrote, and the friends I made. We all dreamed of doing something like this.

Ryan Newman — Right after I sent Picture Perfect to the editor in February of 2020 there was a huge crash at the Daytona NASCAR race. It was devastating to watch, and for a couple of days I wasn't sure that I would ever be watching again. The picture of you walking of the hospital with your daughters was proof of how the safety has changed in the cars. You will forever be my favorite driver.

Julie, Mary, and Val at Books and Mood PR — Thank you for the hard work you have put into promoting Gravity and everything goes with it. You're the best!

You – For taking the time to read my words, and I appreciate that more than anything. Reviews are my best friend if you want to leave one.

About the Author

Sundae Leighton is a romance author who writes sweet stories with a twist. She lives in New England with her husband and cats. She'll tell you she's a coffee snob, enjoys binge watching her favorite shows, loves watching NASCAR, is a bit of a geek at times, an absolute mug hoarder, lover of pumpkin spice, and a complete Jeopardy nerd.

**Don't miss the first book in the Wide Open Series
"Picture Perfect" – available at
shop.sundaeleighton.com
or wherever books are sold.**

Reach Out

All things Sundae Leighton

(new releases, teasers, sneak peaks, email list, social club):
http://www.sundaeleighton.com

Facebook Readers Group:

http://www.facebook.com/groups/233608387885905/

Facebook:

http://www.facebook.com/authorsundaeleighton

Instagram: http://www.instagram.com/sundaeleighton/

Twitter: http://www.twitter.com/sundaeleighton

Goodreads:

http://www.goodreads.com/authorsundaeleighton